Brock grinned and Anya gasped in delight as the dog scooted alongside her leg and began eating from her hand.

Anya beamed at him. "Thank you."

"This is your doing. Not mine." Brock swallowed with great difficulty. "So let me get this straight. When you're not making the best coffee in Aurora, you're helping me with the ski patrol, knitting hats for poor people and rescuing frightened dogs?"

She laughed. "It's only the one."

He handed her a few more treats. "One what?"

"One hat and one dog." She shrugged. "I'm kind of new at this…faith and making a difference."

"It suits you," he said in a voice almost too quiet for her to hear.

Who was he kidding? This was more than just business.

He hadn't asked for it, but Anya had crawled under his skin. His reluctance to admit it didn't change the fact that they were becoming friends.

Close friends.

Books by Teri Wilson

Love Inspired

Alaskan Hearts
Alaskan Hero

TERI WILSON

grew up as an only child and could often be found with her head in a book, lost in a world of heroes, heroines and exotic places. As an adult, her love of books has led her to her dream career—writing. Now an award-winning author of inspirational romance, Teri spends as much time as she can seeing exotic places for herself, then coming home and writing about them, of course. When she isn't traveling or spending quality time with her laptop, she enjoys baking cupcakes, going to movies and hanging out with her family, friends and five dogs. Teri lives in San Antonio, Texas, and loves to hear from readers. She can be contacted via her website at www.teriwilson.net.

Alaskan Hero
Teri Wilson

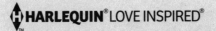

HARLEQUIN® LOVE INSPIRED®

Recycling programs
for this product may
not exist in your area.

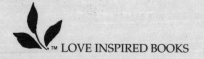

™ LOVE INSPIRED BOOKS

ISBN-13: 978-0-373-81695-8

ALASKAN HERO

www.LoveInspiredBooks.com

Printed in U.S.A.

Though the mountains be shaken
and the hills be removed, yet my unfailing love
for you will not be shaken.
—*Isaiah* 54:10

In loving memory of Robert K. Wilson, Sr.,
my grandpa and a real-life hero.

This book is also dedicated to
the men, women and dogs involved with
search and rescue all over the world.

Acknowledgments

Special thanks to Beckie Ugolini, for her support,
friendship and the idea for Brock's bear suit.
Also, thanks to Meg Benjamin, my writing friend,
RWA roommate and awesome critique partner.

As always, I owe a debt of gratitude to my fantastic
agent, Elizabeth Winick. And I'm blessed
with the best editors in the world,
Rachel Burkot and Melissa Endlich.

Thank you to my loving and supportive family.

Thank you to the people of Alaska
and the Iditarod Trail Dog Sled Race for a
bottomless well of inspiration: Emil Churchin,
Hugh Neff, Deby Trosper, Kate Swift and
especially Zoya DeNure, for giving me the
"the odds are good, but the goods are odd" line.
And Silvia Furtwaengler for giving me the ride
of my life at Iditarod 2012.

Thank you to Elizabeth Chambers and everyone
at Bird Bakery, for giving me a fun place to write
and for the many, many cupcakes.

And last but not least, thank you
Wendy Pohlhammer for creating the pattern
for Brock's hat and for doing the impossible—
teaching me how to knit.

Chapter One

Anya Petrova shoved her mittened hands in the pockets of her parka as she stood on Brock Parker's threshold and tried not to react. The man had answered the door dressed in a furry bear costume. It wasn't every day that she knocked on a stranger's door and found a grizzly bear, albeit a fake one, on the other side. Even in Alaska.

She pasted on a smile. "Hi, I'm Anya Petrova. I emailed you about my dog. You're Brock, right?"

He nodded, but made no move to take off the bear head.

Super. Anya had to stop herself from exhaling a frustrated sigh.

She'd expected someone normal, especially considering Brock Parker's reputation. He was new in town, an avalanche search and rescue expert and alleged dog genius, at least according to what Anya's friend Clementine had told her. Anya had been trying in vain to reach him for the past two days, but he appeared to be a mystery. He didn't even have a locally listed phone number, and he'd yet to make an appearance in town. And she'd been looking— hard—because a dog genius is exactly what she needed at the moment.

Fortunately, Clementine had managed to procure Brock's email address. Anya had fired off a message and was thrilled when he agreed to meet with her. Clementine had predicted he would turn out to be the answer to Anya's prayers. What she'd failed to predict was that Brock Parker would be dressed head to toe in a grizzly bear costume when he answered his front door.

The odds are good, but the goods are odd.

Some considered it Alaska's best kept secret.

The rest of the free world seemed all too aware of the fact that men outnumbered women in the Land of the Midnight Sun. So much so that sometimes the statistics Anya Petrova saw on the subject made her shake her head in disbelief, if not snort with laughter. Fifteen to one? Did people in the Lower 48 really believe that?

Anya had lived in Aurora, Alaska, since the day she was born. She even had a dash of Inuit blood in her veins, and she knew as well as every other Alaskan woman that such statistics were exaggerated at best. At worst, they were baloney. In any event, the exact ratio didn't make a bit of difference. Because the men of Alaska weren't like other men. The majority of them, anyway. Like anything else, there were exceptions.

A few.

A *very* few.

The odds are good, but the goods are odd. Or, to put it nicely, Alaskan men could be eccentric. And it wasn't just the locals. Sometimes the transplants could be even worse. There seemed to be something about Alaska that attracted independent spirits, adventurers…and oddballs. Case in point—the man standing in front of her in a bear costume.

Not that she cared a whit about Aurora's bachelor population, strange or otherwise. She'd learned a long time ago that men were trouble. In her infancy, actually. Being abandoned by her father at three months of age didn't exactly set her up for success in the man department. Neither did being unceremoniously dumped on top of the highest mountain in Aurora for the entire town to witness. More than the town's population, actually, because television cameras had been involved.

As a result, dating wasn't anywhere on the list of things that mattered most to Anya. Her life was simple. She cared about three things—God, coffee and her dog.

She had a good handle on the coffee situation. As the manager of the Northern Lights Inn coffee bar, she was given free rein to develop all sorts of lattes, mochas and espresso drinks. Whatever struck her fancy, really. She enjoyed it. And she was good at it. Sometimes—particularly on days when all she did was serve up cup after cup of plain black coffee— she wondered if there was something else she should be doing with her life. Something more meaningful. But that was normal, wasn't it? Did people really ever feel completely fulfilled by their jobs?

The God thing was new, so she really couldn't say how that was going. But it mattered to her. More than she ever knew it could, so it went on the list.

But the dog was another issue entirely. And that's where Brock Parker came into the picture, or so Anya hoped. Clementine had been so sure he could help her. She'd used the word *genius* to describe his proficiency at training.

He sure didn't look like a genius standing there in his doorway in that bear costume. Then again, what did Anya know about geniuses? Hadn't she read somewhere that Albert Einstein couldn't tie his own shoes? Maybe Einstein had a bear suit too.

She glanced down at Brock's feet poking out from the dark-brown fur. He wore hiking boots, and they were indeed tied.

Was that a good thing? Who knew?

She inhaled a deep breath of frigid winter air and tried again. "I have a very anxious dog, and I was told you might be able to help me. I'm kind of desperate."

She'd planned to tell him more, but suddenly her eyes burned with the telltale sting of tears. To say she was desperate was an understatement. Things seemed bad enough when she'd first rescued Dolce. The poor thing hid under the bed all the time. Anya barely saw her. Little did she know Dolce's shyness was the least of her problems.

The tiny dog also howled at the top of her canine lungs. At first, Anya had been able to convince the people at the Northern Lights Inn—who were not only her employer, but also her landlord—to give the dog some time. Surely Dolce would settle down.

She hadn't. Not yet anyway. And the hotel management had run out of patience. They'd finally given her an ultimatum—give up either the dog or her rent-free cottage.

The choice was hers. She had a mere fourteen days to fix the problem or lose her dog or her home. She'd pinned her last hope on Brock's purported genius, and from the looks of things, that might have been a mistake.

She sniffed and willed herself not to shed a tear. Desperate or not, crying in front of a man dressed as a bear was simply out of the question.

She heard a sigh. Brock's furry chest rose and fell. Then—*finally*—he removed the bear head, exposing his face.

Anya wasn't altogether sure what she'd expected, but the cool blue eyes, straight perfect nose and high cheekbones that looked as though they'd been chiseled from granite were most definitely not it. The man resembled some kind of dreamy Nordic statue. Anya had to blink to make sure she wasn't seeing things.

"You say your dog is anxious? How anxious?" He spoke without cracking the slightest smile, which only made him look more like something Michelangelo had carved out of stone.

Anya swallowed. Her mouth had abruptly gone dry. The snowflakes floating against her cheeks felt colder all of a sudden, and she realized her face had grown quite warm. "Very. I rescued her from a bad situation, and unless she's attached to a leash, I can't get her to come out from under my bed. She even eats there and only in the dark."

It was pathetic. Every night when Anya drifted off to sleep, it was to the sound of poor Dolce crunching on kibble.

"But that's not the worst of it. She howls. Rather loudly." Anya's voice grew wobbly. "I'm about to be kicked out of my cottage."

"I see." Brock nodded, and a lock of his disheveled blond hair fell across his forehead.

She'd heard of bedhead, but never *bear*head. It, too, appeared to have its charms.

A shiver ran up Anya's spine—a shiver she attributed to the fact that she was still standing on his front porch and the temperature had dipped well below freezing.

Yeah, right.

"Come with me." Still clutching the bear head under his arm, he led her inside.

Anya had been in the house once, long before she'd ever heard of Brock. She'd babysat nine-year-old twins who had lived here when she was in high school. Other than Brock's array of unopened moving boxes, the living room looked pretty much the same—wood floors, dark paneled walls and huge floor-to-ceiling windows overlooking the rugged, snow-capped Chugach Mountain range. The view was breathtaking, even to Anya, who'd seen the splendors of Alaska virtually every day of her life.

Brock strode past the window with barely a glance, leading her through the dining room and kitchen and out the back door. The snow crunched beneath their feet as they headed toward a barnlike structure about a dozen yards from the house. The barn was new—at least it hadn't been part of the landscape when the Davis twins were nine. If there was a walkway, it wasn't visible beneath the previous night's snowfall. Flurries were still coming down, swirling and drifting through the branches of the evergreen trees. By the time they reached the barn, the shoulders of Brock's bear costume were dusted with a fine layer of white.

"This is my training area." He pushed the door open with a grizzly paw and ushered her inside.

The smell of sawdust and puppies drifted to Anya's nostrils. A strange combination, but not at all unpleasant. In fact, she found it oddly comforting. "Wow. Nice."

Calling it a barn wasn't really fair. The word barn conjured up images of dirty, hay-strewn floors and farming equipment covered in layers of dust. This building had been swept and cleaned to the point of perfection. A series of short, wooden dividers separated the center of the room into four pens. What Anya assumed was leftover lumber had been stacked neatly against the wall. Brock may have been new in town, but clearly he'd been busy.

Above the excess planks of wood were a series of hooks. What looked like a ski patrol jacket hung from one of them. Anya's gaze lingered on the bright-red parka and moved over the intersecting lines of the bold white cross printed on it until Brock spoke again, stealing her attention.

"Sit there." He pointed to one of the square, wood-framed pens.

Anya glanced at him, wishing he would offer more of an explanation. She didn't see a chair anywhere. What was she supposed to do? Sit on the floor? But as she approached the box, a cute, furry head peeked over one of the short walls. Then another equally adorable face popped up beside it.

"Puppies!" Anya clapped her hands.

She swung her leg over the short wall and climbed inside with the dogs, sitting cross-legged in the center of the pen. One of the puppies immediately crawled into her lap, but the other one eyed her from a foot or two away.

They didn't look like any puppies Anya had ever seen, certainly not the customary sled dogs that populated Alaska. These were a lovely red color, with white markings on their feet and chests.

"What kind of dogs are these?" she asked. "They almost look like little foxes."

"Nova Scotia Duck Tolling Retrievers," Brock said, as if that mouthful of an answer made a lick of sense to Anya. He reached for a newspaper that was folded and placed neatly on one of the wooden dividers and handed it to her. "I'd like you to read this."

She glanced at the paper, this morning's edition of the *Yukon Reporter*. She scanned the front page for anything dog-related but came up empty. "Um, what exactly am I supposed to be reading?"

He shrugged what appeared to be a rather muscular shoulder, visible even through the bear suit. "It doesn't matter. Just read it."

"Okaaay." She gave him a wary glance, but the look on his face told her nothing. He still wore that same stony expression. Stony, but undeniably handsome.

She unfolded the paper. The headline had something to do with the ski resort. Anya skipped over that particular article. Intentionally. Although the ski mountain loomed over Aurora, Anya had managed to pretty much ignore it since the day she'd had her heart broken atop it. She instead found a story about a moose that had been spotted roaming the streets of downtown after dark.

The moose, a young adult bull according to eye-witnesses, is thought to be the cause of recent...

Brock's deep voice interrupted her train of thought. "Out loud."

"Out loud?" Anya raised her brows and looked back down at the newspaper, then at the two puppies with their sweet little fox-like faces, and back at Brock. "You want me to read the newspaper to the dogs?"

"Yep." He nodded, crossed his big bear arms and waited.

Odd, she decided. *Most definitely.*

But she couldn't deny he was odd in a rather intriguing way.

She resumed reading, aloud this time, acutely aware of those glacial blue eyes watching her. Her cheeks grew warm, and she had to concentrate so her tongue wouldn't trip on the words. Those flawless good looks of his were unnerving. Not that she was attracted to him, because she wasn't. Of course she wasn't. He made her nervous, that's all.

Still, she almost wished he'd cover up his perfect bone structure with that silly bear head.

Brock watched Anya read to the pups until she'd finished the article about the rogue moose that was vandalizing downtown Aurora. Not that there was much of a downtown, he mused. Certainly not compared to Seattle, where he'd lived for the past year and a half. There wasn't a Starbucks or a Seattle's Best anywhere in sight.

"...authorities are asking anyone who sees the moose to contact Wildlife Care and Control." Anya paused and blinked up at him with the most beautiful eyes he'd ever seen.

Brock ignored the zing they sent straight to his chest and nodded. She started on another article, something about a rehabilitated sea otter being released into nearby Kachemak Bay.

Brock shook his head and marveled at the fact that he'd somehow landed in a place where moose and sea otters made the front page of the local paper. To top it off, he was sweltering in the grizzly suit. It was the dead of winter in Alaska, but the barn was heated and he was used to the cold. Brock had spent the better part of his adult life in the snow—if not actively searching for avalanche victims, then training for the inevitable event of a slide.

He left Anya to her reading and went to change. The two pups had settled around her comfortably, even Sherlock, the more cautious of the pair. Brock was pleased. The aim of the whole newspaper exercise was to socialize the young dogs to new people, new voices. The bear suit was a similar tool for socialization training. The dogs would be living in Alaska. They needed to be prepared for the sight of bears when they were out on the mountain training for search and rescue.

Sherlock had warmed to Anya faster than he'd anticipated. It wasn't often that Brock had a woman around to assist with training. Then again, Anya's voice had a pleasant, lyrical quality about it. Who wouldn't warm to the sound of that?

He frowned as he headed back to the house. This was why he'd hesitated when Anya Petrova had shown up on his doorstep asking for help with her dog—unexpected pleasantries, such as the sound of a feminine voice and a pair of eyes the exact color of Rocky Mountain lavender, only complicated things.

Since the disappearance of his brother when Brock was a child, he'd worked hard to keep people at arm's length. It was a necessary life skill for an eight-year-old boy who'd come to learn that sometimes people vanished. And they never came home.

As an adult, he'd devoted his life to finding the missing so other families could avoid the pain and uncertainty his own had experienced. But that's where his relationships most often ended. After the find. He'd seen the pain that losing a loved one caused. He'd lived it. And he honestly didn't think he had it in him to live it again. So he structured his life in a way that ensured he wouldn't.

But it had been those eyes of hers that convinced him to open the door.

He'd never seen eyes that color—such an intense shade of violet. They brought to mind a vineyard. Or a field of wildflowers. Or a dozen other romantic notions that Brock would rather not think about.

He huffed out an exhale and stalked back toward the barn, clad now in jeans and a Search and Rescue sweatshirt instead of the oppressive bear suit. He was overthinking things. She could help him with the pups he'd promised to train and provide for Aurora's inaugural Avalanche Search and Rescue Canine Unit, and in the process, he'd teach her how to help her timid dog. It was a win–win situation for both of them. How complicated could it get?

Anya had moved on to the sports page by the time Brock returned to the training area. He milled about, organizing probe poles and checking the batteries in his assortment of beacons as she enlightened the pups on the latest developments in the local curling club.

Curling had made the sports section? Seriously? Brock was still trying to wrap his mind around the fact that it was now an Olympic sport. He stifled a grin.

As things went, having her around wasn't so bad.

He glanced at his Swiss Army watch and decided to let her keep going for another ten minutes. In the meantime, he'd put a bit of his leftover wood to good use.

He reached for a small piece, not too much bigger than his hand, and dug around in the pocket of his jeans for his knife. He leaned against the workbench and crossed his feet at the ankles. Then he went to work shaving off the outer layer of the wood, one smooth strip at a time.

His grandfather had taught him how to whittle when he was a kid. It had been the last thing Brock and his brother had learned to do together. Sometimes, when he was feeling introspective, he wondered if that's why he went back to the hobby time and again. Mostly, though, he did it without thinking.

As his knife moved over the wood in rhythm to the rise and fall of Anya's voice, Brock lost himself in the tranquility of the moment. The tension in his shoulders eased. He forgot about the meeting with the current ski patrol members he was expected to lead in the morning and the other myriad things he needed to do in order to get the new unit started on the mountain. He even forgot about the other search he'd been concerned about—the one for a tolerable cup of coffee. He was able to let it all go until her voice stopped.

His hands stilled and his knife paused mid-stroke.

He looked up and found Anya standing before him, her hands planted firmly on her slender hips.

"I've finished." She narrowed her gaze at him.

The full force of those eyes was a bit much for him to take, so he focused instead on her forehead. "You've finished? What do you mean?"

"I mean I've read the entire newspaper aloud to your dogs. They're snoring loud enough to peel the paint off the walls."

"The entire paper? Are you serious?" Brock glanced at his watch. Somehow, what felt like ten minutes had in actuality been closer to an hour and a half.

"Deadly." She swept him up and down with her gaze and bit her bottom lip. "What happened to the bear suit?"

He tossed his chunk of wood—now carved into a nice, smooth sphere—onto the workbench. "It was a bit warm, I'm afraid."

"That's a shame. Perhaps you can find something lighter. I hear faux elk fur is more ventilated."

She was baiting him, clearly angling for an explanation as to why he'd been dressed as a bear when she arrived.

Brock wasn't about to give her the satisfaction. If she'd simply come out and asked, he likely would have. But not now. "My elk suit is at the cleaners."

She rolled her eyes, but he could see the trace of

a smile on her lips. "So when do my training lessons start?"

"They already did." He nodded toward the paper, still dangling from her fingertips. "That was your first one."

"And how is reading the newspaper to your puppies all afternoon supposed to get my dog quiet and out from under the bed?" Something close to anger flashed in her amethyst eyes.

Brock chastised himself. What was he doing looking at those eyes again? "That's for you to figure out."

"You're seriously not going to explain it to me?"

"Nope." He smiled, which only seemed to make her more agitated.

He could have spelled it out for her, could have told her to get down on her dog's level and spend time there. Loads of time, doing ordinary things, until the dog became comfortable with her there. But he'd always been a believer in doing instead of telling. People typically learned more if they had to think things through.

"I'm almost afraid to ask what lesson number two will involve." Anya shoved the newspaper at his chest.

He caught it before she spun on her heel and made a beeline for the door.

"Come back at the same time tomorrow and you'll find out," he said to her back.

She turned, and a curtain of amber hair spilled over her shoulder. For the first time, Brock noticed a hint of warm mocha in her skin tone. She shot a parting glance at him, and a jolt of attraction hit Brock so hard that he nearly stumbled backward.

And the way that one captivating look settled in his gut told Brock things were going to get quite a bit more complicated than he'd bargained for.

Chapter Two

Darkness had fallen over Aurora by the time Anya left Brock's house. Of course, this was Alaska, so it had likely gotten dark shortly after 4:30—probably around the time she'd been reading the curling scores to Brock's sleeping dogs.

Now it was nearly six o'clock, which meant she'd have to head straight to church or she'd be late for knitting group. She'd hoped to have time to run home and let Dolce out first. A familiar wave of panic washed over her when she thought of the mournful howls that were likely emanating from her cottage.

Anya let out a huff of frustration. By now she thought she'd have some inkling as to what to do about the ongoing Dolce problem. But, although an entire afternoon spent at the dog genius's home had proved interesting, to say the least, she was just as clueless as ever.

Clueless, but still determined to get through to the dog. Giving up wasn't an option.

The first time Anya had seen Dolce, the poor dog was being kicked in the ribs. She'd watched, horrified, from the window at the coffee shop where she worked at the Northern Lights Inn, convinced what she was seeing wasn't real…until the little dog let out a yelp.

Then she'd marched right outside and confronted the abuser. He'd been huge, easily a foot taller and nearly twice as broad as Anya. He'd also been more than a little drunk, which was no excuse for mistreating an animal. Anya had wedged herself between dog and man, crossed her arms and told him to behave himself or she'd call the police. She could only attribute the fact that he'd gone still to the frantic prayers she'd been uttering under her breath. Or perhaps, in his drunken haze, he'd seen two or three of her. A whole group of angry females instead of only one. Her heart had just about beat right out of her chest as she stood there, fully expecting the man to unleash his fury on her in place of his dog. In the end, he'd stumbled away, abandoning the pup without a parting glance.

And Anya had suddenly found herself with a dog.

She'd made up her mind right then and there to show the dog what love—and a real home—was all about. Something about seeing her shivering out in the cold, beaten down and all alone in the world, reminded Anya of herself as a baby. She'd never been abused, thank goodness. And she'd had her mother, of course, even after her father had walked out. But her mother had been too caught up in the bitterness of being left to provide much comfort to Anya, even as she grew into a young woman.

Anya knew better than to fantasize about changing the past, but she could change the future. At least for Dolce. She wouldn't abandon her now, even if things were less than ideal.

But if Dolce didn't get over her anxiety soon, Anya might not have a choice in the matter. In addition to being only marginally fulfilling, working as a barista also meant she was only marginally solvent. She couldn't afford to move out of her rent-free cottage.

Her disappointment in the first "training session" with Brock ebbed somewhat as she put on her parking brake and headed inside Aurora Community Church's Fellowship Hall. Even though she'd been attending church regularly for several months now, the feeling of peace evoked by simply walking through the front door never failed to catch her by surprise. She'd spent many years uncomfortable with even the mention of God. Something about growing up with an absent dad didn't exactly inspire confidence in a God known to most as God the Father.

When Clementine, an avid churchgoer, had moved to Aurora and she and Anya became fast friends, the invitations to church events came rolling in. Anya managed to decline each one politely yet succinctly. Then Clementine's husband, Ben, left town for two weeks to mush his dog sledding team in a race out by Fairbanks. Anya's resistance wavered at the thought of Clementine sitting in a pew alone, so she finally gave in. And that day the pastor had read a verse from the Bible that had stolen the breath from Anya's lungs.

Never will I leave you; never will I forsake you.

Anya had experienced her fair share of leaving. The holy words had hit her square in the chest and burrowed deep inside. They'd danced in her thoughts all week until she found herself back in the pew the following Sunday. And the Sunday after that—the day she'd rescued Dolce. She'd known at once the timing of saving her couldn't be a coincidence. For the first time, she felt as though she'd been put somewhere for a reason.

And here she was now, headed to church again. On a Monday night, no less.

"Anya, hi."

"Hey, Anya."

A chorus of hellos rose up to greet her as she breezed into the fellowship hall, a former gymnasium the church now used for casual events such as youth group meetings and potluck suppers. And knitting, of course. She waved at the half-dozen women gathered around the long, rectangular table situated in the center of the room and found a seat between Clementine and Sue Chase. Like Clementine, Sue was a musher's wife. The two of them were long-time Christians. Not babies in the faith, as Anya sometimes thought of herself. They were very involved in organizing ways to help the community. In fact, the knitting group had been Sue's idea.

"Good evening, ladies," Sue said, and the clickety-clack of knitting needles came to a stop.

Anya pulled her own needles and ball of yarn out of her tote bag as she listened.

"Next week, Gus is taking a couple of volunteer doctors out to the Bush to treat people in some of the more impoverished villages." Sue absently wound a length of red yarn around her fingers.

Gus was the manager of Aurora's one and only grocery store. He was also a pilot who made regular runs out to the Bush, the area of Alaska that was off the road network and inaccessible by car.

"I'd love it if we could get together at least two dozen hats to send along. So far we have twenty." Sue's gaze flitted around the table. "Do you all think we could get together four more before next week?"

"I'm almost finished with mine." Clementine held up a nearly complete hat, crafted of pink yarn sprinkled with sequins.

Anya couldn't help but laugh. It was classic Clementine.

"What's so funny?" Clementine whispered.

"Nothing." Anya shrugged. "I hope the underprivileged like sparkle, that's all."

Clementine looked down at her hat. "Of course they do. Doesn't everyone?"

Anya's hat was a bit simpler, crafted of a fuzzy plum-colored yarn. She was a baby knitter, in addition to being a baby Christian. Finishing her hat by next week would be a challenge, but she really liked the idea of keeping someone warm in a cold Alaskan winter. Since discovering God, Anya was trying to make her life count for something. Something bigger than herself. Saving Dolce was only the start.

She'd need to start knitting at home to get caught up. She bit her lip and went to work wrapping the yarn around her needles.

"Oh." Clementine's hands stopped moving. "I almost forgot to ask. Did you make it out to Brock Parker's house today?"

Anya frowned. "I sure did." She hadn't meant to inject an edge to her voice, but there it was.

Clementine's knitting dropped to her lap. "What's wrong?"

"Nothing."

"That row you just purled is so tight, it's about to snap in two. Something's most definitely wrong."

Ugh, she was right. The row was way too snug. Anya unraveled it. "Nothing's wrong. Brock Parker is a crazy man, that's all."

"Crazy?" Clementine tilted her head. "Are you sure? He's kind of a big deal, you know."

"A big deal? How?" Unless she meant big as in

tall and rather strapping—*ahem*—Anya wasn't sure what she was talking about.

"He's pretty famous. He goes all over the world setting up special canine rescue teams for areas prone to avalanches. And Ben says he's found dozens of people who got caught in slides. You should Google him."

Anya raised her brows. "Does Google mention that he enjoys dressing as a bear?"

"What?"

"You heard me. He was wearing a grizzly bear suit when I got there."

"That does sound odd." Clementine paused. "But did he say he'd help you with Dolce?"

"Yes. I had my first lesson today." Anya used air quotes to emphasize the word *lesson.*

"Oh, great!" Clementine beamed. "What was it like?"

"He had me read the entire newspaper aloud to his two puppies."

"The whole front page?" The smile on Clementine's face dimmed, replaced with a look of confusion.

Join the club, Anya thought. "Every section, not just the front page. The whole *paper.* I almost lost my voice."

"Hmm. What was he doing while you read the paper?"

"He was whittling. *Whittling.*" Anya shook her head. The entire episode sounded completely unbelievable, even to her own ears. And she'd actually been there. "Who does that?"

Beside her, Clementine's shoulders shook with laughter. "I hear that guy from Nome who always drives around with a reindeer in the bed of his pickup truck likes to carve things out of sheep horns."

"My point exactly," Anya huffed.

It wasn't the whittling. It wasn't the mysterious, unexplained reading-to-the-dogs assignment. It wasn't even the bear suit. It was all of it put together.

Brock Parker was one unusual package.

So why did her heart seem to kick into overdrive at the mere thought of him?

Clementine narrowed her gaze at her, as if trying to see inside her head. "What does he look like?"

Anya's fingers slipped, and she dropped a stitch in the hat she was knitting.

Oops.

"Um," she started, as her face flushed with warmth.

"I see." Sue laughed. "He looks that good, huh?"

Anya hadn't even realized Sue had been paying attention to their conversation. She wanted to crawl under the table and hide. Clearly that wasn't an option, seeing as Sue and Clementine were watching her with great interest. Her fingers fumbled once more, and she dropped another stitch. Darn it. She'd never finish the hat at this rate.

She decided to go ahead and fess up. They'd find out eventually.

"He's blond, blue-eyed and Nordic looking." She cleared her throat. "Not that it matters."

"Nordic looking?" Clementine lifted an inquisitive brow.

"You know, like a Viking or something." Anya ignored the flush still simmering in her cheeks and focused intently on her knitting. "Like I said, it doesn't make a bit of difference."

"Of course it doesn't," Sue said, tongue firmly planted in cheek.

Anya looked up from her tangle of yarn and sighed. "Seriously, you two. Other than what he can do for my dog, I have no interest in Brock Parker."

In fact, things would probably be easier if he wasn't so flawlessly handsome. Because in the end—no matter what they looked like—all men did the same thing. At least the ones Anya had known. They left.

"Seriously," she repeated for emphasis. "You both know I don't date."

Clementine's fingers stilled, and her yarn stopped moving. "Wait. We do?"

"Of course you do," Anya said.

Clementine hadn't yet moved to Aurora when Anya was dumped on national television, but Anya was certain she'd mentioned it to her during the course of their friendship.

"No, I don't." Clementine shook her head. "You don't date? What on Earth does that mean?"

Okay, so maybe she hadn't mentioned it. Although it was a pivotal moment in her life to be sure, it wasn't exactly the sort of thing she revisited often. Or ever, really.

Anya sighed. "I had a rather ugly breakup a few years ago, that's all."

"How ugly?" Clementine frowned and glanced back and forth between Anya and Sue.

"It was televised," Sue chimed in, much to Anya's relief. She'd rather not be forced to tell the entire dreadful tale herself.

Clementine furrowed her brow. "How does a breakup end up on television?"

"I was dating my high school sweetheart, who was a champion skier. A downhill racer."

"Speed Lawson," Sue said.

"Speed?" Clementine snorted. "What kind of a name is Speed?"

"The kind for men who beat a hasty trail out of town when the opportunity arises." Anya's gaze bore into her knitting. Maybe if she concentrated on the in-and-out of her needles and the twisting of the yarn around her fingers, she could get through this with a modicum of dignity still intact.

"Is that what happened? He just up and left?" Clementine rested a hand on top of Anya's.

"We'd been dating two years when the Olympic Trials came to Aurora. The night before his event,

Speed told me he loved me and wanted us to build a life together."

Anya still felt ridiculous when she thought about it—the night she'd poured her heart into that boy in a way only a girl who'd never known the love of a father could. And he'd thrown it away. For all the world to see.

"What happened?" Clementine cast a worried glance at Sue.

"He made the team as an alternate," Sue said. "It was big news around here."

"The biggest." Anya nodded. "ESPN interviewed him afterward, right there on the mountain. They asked him about skiing, living in Alaska, the ordinary questions…then they wanted to know if he had a girlfriend or any plans for the future."

"And what did he say?" Clementine lowered her voice to a near whisper.

Anya appreciated the gesture, but it didn't matter. Everyone sitting at the table knew the story. Was there a soul in Aurora who didn't? "He said, and I quote, 'There's no one special.'"

"Oh, Anya. He was young. Don't you think they may have caught him off guard?" Clementine's word echoed every desperate thought that had entered Anya's head in the aftermath of the interview.

She'd stood right there, hurt and humiliated, with the rest of Speed's hometown crowd and listened to him deny her very existence. She'd pretended that the tears streaming down her cheeks were a product of the cold Alaskan wind rather than the pain of her heart breaking. But she hadn't fooled anyone, least of all herself.

Worse than that, in the instant he'd uttered those words—*no one special*—something inside her had turned hard and bitter. Just like her mother.

It was that dark thing she felt brewing inside that frightened her the most. So she'd done the only thing she knew to keep it at bay. She stayed as far away from men as she could.

"I never heard from him again," Anya said tersely. She left out the part about the local media questioning her about Speed's comments and the *Yukon Reporter* article that had called her Speed's "*brokenhearted hometown honey.*" Clementine knew enough now to get the picture. "And that's why I don't date. Anyone. Most especially a hotshot like Brock Parker."

"Well, I for one hope you give the lessons with Brock another chance." Sue gave her shoulder a pat before rising and heading to help one of the knitters who seemed to be having trouble casting off.

"Me too." Clementine nodded. "I'm sure he can help Dolce. There has to be a method to his madness."

A method to his madness.

Anya turned the phrase over in her mind. He was

mad all right. She just hoped there was a method involved. That's what really mattered, not his looks.

The fact that those chiseled features of his made her stomach flip was an inconvenience she'd have to grow accustomed to.

That's all.

Brock was forced to trudge through what he estimated to be two and a half feet of snow to get to his truck. He'd shoveled the sidewalk from his front door to the driveway late the night before, but by morning it was once again indistinguishable. Nothing but snow stretched out before him—an unspoiled blanket of white glittering in the morning sunshine.

Welcome to Alaska, he thought as he cranked the truck engine to life.

There was a time when Brock would have found it beautiful, before snow had become an enemy to be conquered. Sometimes he had to struggle to remember how it had felt back then—building a snowman on the first day of winter, snowball fights that left his fingers prickly and numb, sledding down the hill behind his elementary school, shouting out to his brother to be careful of the trees. His memories of childhood snow days were so tangled up with his memories of Drew that it was hard to separate them. Then Drew had disappeared. Taken right from his bedroom window, according to the police. The snow had kept on falling and, inch by inch, swallowed up any evidence that could lead to Drew's whereabouts.

They'd never found Drew, never found who'd taken him. Unable to concentrate his rage and confusion onto an actual person, Brock had instead focused it all on the snow. He supposed in a way, he still did.

He maneuvered his truck through what passed for downtown in Aurora. Nestled between a lake—frozen completely over at the moment, of course—and the foot of the Chugach Mountain range, the hub of the small town appeared to be the Northern Lights Inn. Judging from the staggering number of cars in the parking lot, it was Aurora's hotspot. This struck Brock as odd, considering the ski area boasted its own chalet-type quarters, complete with gingerbread trim and old-world, fairytale charm. He narrowed his gaze at the ordinary-looking hotel, wondering what the draw could possibly be, and turned onto the road leading to the tiny log cabin that served as the Ski Patrol headquarters.

The three full-time members of the Aurora Ski Patrol Unit were already waiting for him when he arrived. They sat around a sturdy wood table that was loaded down with bagels and coffee, grinning at him as if he were the answer to all the town's prayers. Which he probably was.

Brock had never felt comfortable being the object of adoration. And no matter how many finds, no matter how large the number of people he'd saved, he still didn't.

"Good morning," he said and shifted from one booted foot to the other.

"Mr. Parker." The man in the center rose. "I'm Cole Weston, senior member of the ski patrol. We're delighted to have you. Welcome to Aurora."

Brock nodded. He recognized Cole's voice from their numerous telephone conversations. "Call me Brock. Please."

"Of course." Cole smiled and introduced him to the men on either side of him—Luke and Jackson, respectively. "Have a seat, please."

Brock poured himself a cup of coffee and eyed it suspiciously before lowering himself into one of the chairs.

"So how do you like the snow?" Cole, unaware he'd asked a very loaded question, grinned and bobbed his head in the direction of the window where flurries swirled against the pane.

Brock blinked. How was he supposed to come up with an answer to that? He chose not to and took a sip of his coffee instead.

Not bad, he mused. *Not bad at all.*

Hands down, it was the best cup of coffee he'd had since leaving Seattle.

"So Brock, have you given much thought to what we discussed about making your position here in

Aurora permanent?" Cole pushed the plate of bagels toward him.

Brock had to give him credit. Cole had certainly cut to the chase faster than most of the ski resorts where he'd done consultant work. Of those resorts, one hundred percent had offered him permanent positions at one time or another. They typically waited until they'd seen his work firsthand, though. Or at least until he'd finished his first cup of coffee.

"I have to be honest, Cole. Permanent relocation is not something I'm considering at this time."

He swallowed, hoping his answer—which had been fine-tuned through years of practice—didn't constitute a lie. Relocation implied that somewhere out there he had a permanent residence, which he most definitely didn't. Brock didn't do permanent.

"The offer still stands." Cole's gaze flitted briefly to Jackson and Luke, who both nodded their agreement. "We're short-staffed here, and as you know, the mountains surrounding Aurora are made up of miles of avalanche terrain. We could really use your help. Permanently."

There was that word again. Brock shrugged out of his parka. The small room was beginning to feel rather warm. "Don't worry. I've brought with me two fine pups—Sherlock and Aspen—who are coming along nicely with their search and rescue training. They'll both be staying here long term after

I've gone. I'll make sure everything is up and running before I leave. You have my promise on that."

"Very well then." Cole nodded grimly. He looked somewhat resigned, but not as much as Brock would have liked. Something told him he hadn't heard the last of the offer.

Luke crossed his arms and leaned back in his chair. "How long do you estimate it will take to establish an avalanche rescue unit here before you go?"

"It depends. The dogs need a few months to become acclimated to the mountain, and the four of us will need to meet for training exercises daily. All in all, I'd guess you'll be good to go in three or four months. Perhaps sooner."

"Then it looks like we have three or four months to change your mind about staying." Jackson reached for a bagel. "Once you've had a chance to familiarize yourself with the town, you might find that you like it here. Alaska is rather, ah, unique."

"Yea, we've got our annual Reindeer Run coming up. That's always a good time." Luke grinned.

Don't hold your breath.

Brock took another bite of his bagel to stop himself from saying it out loud. Aurora, Alaska, no matter how quaint or picturesque, surely couldn't have more to offer than Banff, Canada, Mont-Tremblant, France, or Cortina, Italy—all places he'd lived in the past two years. And even if he did find something special here, it would probably make him all the more determined to leave.

Unbidden, the memory of Anya Petrova's eyes flashed in Brock's mind. That deep, welcoming violet filled him with a sudden rush of warmth.

He frowned and wondered what that was all about.

Chapter Three

Anya ran her dishcloth in circles over the coffee bar as she peered at the screen of the computer she typically used for ringing up customers. Not so typically, the monitor was now fixed on an image of Brock Parker. Minus the bear suit and standing on a mountaintop overlooking the Swiss Alps, he looked every inch the hero that countless websites professed him to be.

She took in his broad shoulders, apparently strong enough to dig through several feet of hard-packed avalanche snow, if the internet was to be trusted, and tried not to gape. When Brock wasn't whittling or reading aloud to his dogs, he was apparently traveling the world and saving people's lives. Anya was having trouble reconciling this information with the man she'd met the night before. He'd rarely even looked her in the eyes. She'd noticed that he seemed to prefer focusing on her forehead, hardly a habit that bespoke of bravery.

"You missed a spot," a voice called from somewhere beside her.

She tore her gaze from the computer and aimed it at the counter, shiny as a mirror after all her absentminded polishing. Perfect…except hers wasn't the only face she saw looking back at her in the reflection. Brock's heroic image was right there across from hers.

He sent her an upside down wink.

Anya's head flew up, and nearly as quickly, her fingers flew across the computer keyboard. She banged on the keys, willing a different website to flash on the screen. She didn't care which one, so long as it wasn't devoted to Brock.

Why, oh why did I take Clementine's advice and Google Brock?

"Were you just Googling me?"

Anya glanced over at him. His lips were curved into a rare smile, making him even more pleasant to look at. Her knees grew wobbly, which she found more than a little irritating. "No."

"No?" He tilted his head.

"No," she said, a little too emphatically.

"Are you sure? Because that guy looked familiar."

She waved toward the screen, which had somehow landed on the Northern Light Inn's homepage. *Thank You, Jesus.*

"You mean him?" She pointed at the website's picture of a stuffed grizzly bear, one of the many examples of Alaska's finest taxidermy that graced the hotel lobby. "I guess I do see the resemblance."

"Good save." He smiled again and glanced at the actual bear, frozen in a threatening pose on its hind legs and looming beside the coffee bar. "But I know what I saw."

She chose to ignore this comment. Because really, what choice did she have? "What brings you here this afternoon, Brock?"

He paused, taking in the coffee bar with its smooth burled wood counter, the refurbished brushed-nickel Gaggia espresso machine—Anya's pride and joy—and, last but not least, the stuffed bison head that watched over everything from its place overhead. Anya had taken to calling him Spiderman because of the copious amount of cobwebs she was often forced to untangle from his shaggy coat.

Brock's gaze snagged on Spiderman for a beat, then returned to its usual place of concentration—Anya's forehead. "I just came from a meeting up on the mountain where I had a fantastic cup of coffee. Cole Weston told me it came from here."

Anya breathed a sigh of relief, pleased the topic of conversation had moved away from her Google search and onto a more mundane topic. Coffee. "Alaska Klondike Roast. Yep, he came by earlier and picked up a box. It's a local favorite."

"You brewed it?" He narrowed his gaze at her.

"Yes. Why do you look so surprised?"

"No reason." He looked longingly at the grinder, which just so happened to be filled with Alaska Klondike beans. "It was just really good coffee. The best I've had in a while."

Anya's cheeks grew warm. Pathetic. People came in here all the time complimenting her coffee and she didn't get all starry-eyed. It was coffee, not rocket science. Why should it be any different with Brock? Just because he was a hero and had that perfect face...

Ugh. Get a clue. He's just another man. Picture him in that crazy bear suit.

"Would you like a cup?" she asked.

"That would be great."

She poured him a to-go cup, hoping he would get the hint and leave. He took a sip but seemed in no hurry to go.

Super.

Anya went to work washing the tiny collection of coffee cups that had accumulated in the sink behind the counter. She was contemplating washing them again, just to have something nonmale and nonheroic to focus on, when Brock spoke up.

"Is that a flyer for the Reindeer Run?" He pointed to the stack of brochures at the end of the coffee bar.

"Yes. Why?" She bit back a smirk. "Are you thinking of participating?"

He shrugged. "I doubt it. Some of the guys at the ski patrol were talking about it this morning, so the name caught my eye."

"You should do it. Actually, now that I think about it, the Reindeer Run is right up your alley."

He gave her a questioning glance. "Why do you say that?"

"People get really into it. They dress up, wear nutty hats." Anya scrunched her brow in faux concentration. "Call me crazy, but I get the impression that's your sort of thing."

Brock leveled his gaze at her over his cup of coffee—actually looked her right in the eye this time. There was a subtle smile in his eyes, even if it didn't make an appearance on his mouth.

Upon being fully appraised by those glacial blue eyes at last, Anya's first instinct was to look away. She scrubbed at an invisible spot on the counter.

She could feel him watching her. It was unsettling. Unsettling in a weak-in-the-knees sort of manner that Anya was in no way accustomed to dealing with. Even Speed had never made her feel this way—all nervous and fluttery.

After what felt like an eternity, Brock stood. "I'll see you later this evening for your training lesson. Thank you for the coffee."

"Yes, of course." She took the bills he slid across the counter.

"Keep the change."

"Thank you." She folded the money and put it in the pocket of her apron. "Very much."

And as she watched him walk away, she told herself that the bittersweet tug of disappointment she felt had nothing to do with the fact that he'd gone.

"Who was that? I haven't seen him around town before." The voice of Zoey Hathaway, the coffee bar's afternoon barista, dragged Anya away from her thoughts.

Anya blinked at Zoey. She hadn't even noticed her arrival.

"Zoey." She smiled. "Hi. Is it time for your shift already?"

"I'm a little early. This morning was really cloudy, and you know what that means." Zoey pulled a face.

When Zoey wasn't behind the coffee bar at the Northern Lights Inn, she could usually be found flying high above the hotel. She was an aspiring pilot. Unfortunately, the turbulent Alaskan weather made it difficult for her to accumulate the necessary flying hours to get her license.

"Your lesson was postponed again?" Anya asked.

"Yep. I suppose it's just as well, though. I needed to get some work done for the committee I'm heading up at church." Zoey sighed and cast a glance toward the revolving doors where Brock had just disappeared. "Who was that again?"

"Brock Parker." *Just your average hero.* Anya swallowed. "He's new in town."

"Oh, I see." Zoey nodded, her gaze lingering on the doorway.

"You're heading up a committee at church?" Anya asked, eager to change the subject to something other than Brock.

"Yes. We have that big service project coming up—the one to help out widows in the area. I'm head of the committee. I was kind of hoping you might want to be involved?" Zoey slipped an apron over her head and wrapped its ties around her waist.

"The service project. Of course." Anya remembered hearing something about it at knitting group. "Sure, I can help out. I've actually been meaning to talk to someone about that. Is it too late to add a name to the list?"

"Absolutely not. We can use all the help we can get."

"Oh no, this wouldn't be a helper. I was wondering about adding a name to the list of women who need help." Anya's stomach churned at the prospect, but she ignored it.

"It's not too late for that either. We still have a few weeks to plan everything." Zoey pulled a small notepad from the back pocket of her jeans. "Okay, I just need the name to add to the list."

Anya swallowed. Could she really do this? "Her name is Kirima Kunayak. She's my mother."

* * *

"What about purple? You should knit something purple. It would look so pretty with your eyes." Sue held a skein of amethyst yarn up to Anya's cheek and nodded her approval. "Gorgeous. Clementine, come here and take a look."

Clementine crossed the center aisle of the yarn store, balancing three balls of wool in each hand. It would take Anya a year to do something with that much yarn. Either Clementine had been practicing her knitting more frequently than Anya had, or she was about to take up juggling.

"Yes. Definitely." Clementine inspected the purple skein. "And look—it's chunky. You could probably make a scarf out of this in no time."

"No, thank you." Chunky or not, there would be no purple scarf in Anya's future. The last thing she wanted to do was draw attention to her eyes.

With obvious reluctance, Sue put the yarn back in its cubby on the wall of the cozy yarn store. "It's awfully pretty. Are you sure?"

"As sure as I am that decaf is a crime against humanity." Decaf. She shuddered. Really, why bother?

Clementine lifted a brow at Sue. "She's sure."

"I gathered." Sue laughed.

"What are you going to make now that your hat for knitting group is finished? You can't stop knitting altogether or you might forget how." Clementine examined her six balls of yarn. All were various shades of pink, yet she was staring at them as if the choice mystified her.

"I'm not sure yet. What about you?" Anya bit back a smile. "I thought you were going to make something for Ben."

"I am." Clementine nodded.

"Then maybe you should steer clear of pink." Anya plucked the six balls of yarn from Clementine's hands and tossed them back where they belonged. She'd extract a thank you out of Clementine's husband at a later date.

"Point taken." Clementine tore her gaze from the wall of pink cubbies and sighed.

"This is nice. And look—it's on sale." Sue fished a bright ball of lime green out of the bargain bin, which was actually a white wicker basket that perfectly showcased the cheery hodgepodge of colors buried inside.

"Now that I like." Anya held out her hand and caught the ball of yarn as Sue tossed it to her.

"Better than decaf?" Clementine asked, her lips quirking into a wry smile.

"Much."

"There's only one ball of it, though. And it's awfully small. You might not be able to finish whatever you decide to start," Sue said.

"I'm sure I can come up with something." Anya clutched the lime-green yarn in her hand and picked a few more balls from the bargain bin—strawberry red, turquoise and tangerine.

Clementine looked on with what appeared to be mounting horror. "I hope you're not planning on using all of those together. That would make one ugly hat."

"Maybe." Anya shrugged. "You never know."

"Wow. Just…wow."

"Anya, is everything okay?" Sue wrapped an arm around Anya's shoulders. "You seem quiet. And Clementine's right—all those yarns would make an awfully odd-looking hat. Should we be worried about you?"

Anya couldn't help but laugh at the crazy assortment of colors in her arms. "I suppose I might be a little distracted. I added my mom's name to the list for the church service project today."

"That was thoughtful," Clementine said.

"I'm glad you think so." Anya blew out a breath. "But I doubt my mother will see it that way."

Sue cocked her head. "No?"

"No. Most definitely not." Anya almost wished she could turn back time to this morning. Then she wouldn't be obsessing over adding her mother's name to this list.

And maybe you wouldn't get caught Googling Brock.

There he was again. Brock. Invading her thoughts.

He was proving to be quite the irritation, even when he wasn't around.

"I should probably get going. There are two puppies at Brock Parker's house that are probably waiting for me to read them the paper. Or *War & Peace* maybe." Anya rolled her eyes.

Clementine led the way as their trio headed toward the register. "I don't understand. Isn't the whole point to help people? What could your mother have against someone helping her?"

"She'll find something. Trust me." Anya lined up her balls of yarn on the counter, catching the lime-green ball just as it was about to roll off the edge.

"If you're really worried about it, I could talk to the committee. We could get her name taken off the list and it would be no problem," Sue said.

She had a point. Zoey was heading up the committee. Anya could just ask her to remove her mother's name from the list, and she wouldn't have a thing to worry about. Other than the pesky matter of the six inches of ice that had accumulated on her mother's roof.

"No. Believe me, she could use the help." Anya shook her head. "Convincing my mother just how much she needs it is the tricky part."

Both the Dolce problem and what to do with the random assortment of yarn she'd just purchased paled in comparison.

Chapter Four

"Aspen and Sherlock are all caught up on the local happenings. Now what?" Anya handed the newspaper to Brock. Thankfully, he'd asked her to keep an eye on the clock this go-round. Just as she suspected, thirty minutes was enough time to cover most everything that went on in Aurora.

It was also apparently enough time for Brock to turn yesterday's smooth sphere of wood into something vaguely resembling a dog.

"Oh, wow." She plucked the tiny figure off the workbench, where it sat amid a small pile of wood shavings. "This is really great. Where did you learn how to do this?"

"My grandfather taught me years ago. It kind of stuck with me." He frowned slightly as he watched her handle the little wooden dog, as if he himself was surprised at what he'd accomplished while she read to the pups.

Anya was surprised herself—surprised he'd actually answered her question. He was a man of few words, after all. She'd finally broken down and asked him about the puppies' names this time, too, because he'd never mentioned them during her first "lesson."

What didn't surprise her, however, was the pair of antlers protruding from the sides of Brock's baseball cap. They were soft and squishy, crafted of brown felt and ridiculously oversized. The get-up wasn't quite as elaborate as his bear suit, but it made a statement nonetheless.

She ducked as he turned his head. "Watch it. You almost poked my eye out with one of your antlers just now."

"Sorry," he said to her forehead.

Anya tried not to think about the fact that he looked so ridiculous in the hat that he bordered on adorable. "So what next?"

"I'd like you to feed them." He nodded toward a large plastic bin situated neatly beneath the workbench. "The kibble is in there. They get about two handfuls each."

She reached down and lifted the lid of the bin. "Where are their bowls?"

He shook his antlered head. "No bowls."

"What do you mean no bowls?" Anya frowned at the tiny pieces of kibble. "You want me to feed them by hand?"

"Piece by piece," Brock called over his shoulder as he left the training room to do who knows what in the house. Perhaps he was going to tackle those untouched moving boxes that still littered his living room. "See? You're learning already."

Perhaps.

Anya was pretty sure she was on her way to figuring out the method to his madness, as Clementine had put it. After she'd gotten home from church the night before, she'd sat down right next to Dolce's hiding spot. If Brock wasn't going to tell her what she should do, she'd just have to emulate what she did at training class.

She hadn't had it in her to read the paper again, so she'd worked on the hat she was knitting instead. After a quarter of an hour, Dolce's anxious whimpering had quieted down. By the time Anya had knitted the final row—nearly two hours after she'd gotten home—she was rewarded with the sight of Dolce's little black nose poking out from beneath the edge of the duvet. It was a first. Most would consider it a small victory at best, but Anya had been delighted.

Now, as Aspen's soft muzzle tickled the palm of Anya's hand in search of more food, she wondered how on Earth she could manage to hand-feed Dolce. She'd probably have to stick her hand under the bed. And turn the lights off. It sounded complicated. But do-able. Definitely do-able.

Brock strolled back in just as the dogs finished the last of their kibble. "How's it going over there?"

"All finished." Anya rose and climbed out of the pen. "For the record, I know what you're doing."

This seemed to get his attention. He angled his head toward her, antlers and all, and looked her square in the eyes. Anya had to remind herself to breathe. It was ridiculous. Men in silly hats shouldn't be able to make women breathless.

"And what is that?" he asked.

"You're Mr. Miyagi-ing me." She wiggled her nose and realized she smelled like dog food.

"Mr. Who?"

"Mr. Miyagi," she repeated. "You know—wax on, wax off."

She waved her hands in the universal wax-on, wax-off gesture. At least, she *thought* it was universal. The look on Brock's face told her otherwise.

He crossed his arms. "I have no idea what you're talking about."

"Wax on, wax off." She circled her hands in the air again. "From *The Karate Kid* movie."

He narrowed his gaze at her. "The one from the eighties, or the one with Will Smith's kid?"

"The one from the eighties, of course." She rolled her eyes. "Please. You don't remake perfection."

He laughed. Anya was fairly certain she'd never heard him laugh before. Surely she would have remembered the way the deep, rumbling sound of it seemed to tickle her insides.

She straightened. "You know the story of the Karate Kid, right? The old man uses household chores to teach his young protégé karate skills and valuable life lessons."

"Am I to assume that I'm the old man in this scenario?"

"Of course." Anya nodded as if the answer was obvious. As if Brock resembled an old man in any way, which he most definitely did not.

He took a step closer to her. "And you're the young, cute protégé, I take it?"

She'd never said *cute*. She was sure of it. "Y-yes."

"And what about the bear costume? And the hat?" He gestured toward his head. "How do they come into the picture?"

"Um…" Anya opened her mouth and promptly closed it. She was still stuck on the matter of Brock's choice of attire.

"They're socialization tools."

"Socialization tools," Anya repeated.

He gestured toward Sherlock and Aspen. "Search and rescue dogs see all sorts of things on the mountain. They need to be unflappable, prepared for anything."

Like men dressed as bears? Right. "Yeah, I doubt that."

Brock lifted a brow. Clearly the genius wasn't

accustomed to being questioned. "Excuse me? You doubt that?"

"I don't think it has anything to do with the dogs. I think you just enjoy dressing this way." She was only half-joking.

Brock's lips curved into a self-deprecating smirk. "Is that so?"

"Oh, yes." She nodded and considered how absolutely perfect he would look in a Viking hat. Perhaps she could find one somewhere.

"I'm curious." His eyes danced with amusement. "How did you figure all this out? Did you learn it on Google earlier?"

Was he ever going to let that go?

"I did not Google you." Anya planted her hands on her hips. *Jesus, forgive me for lying.*

"We both know you did." The corner of his mouth lifted into a knowing grin.

The ground didn't open her up and swallow her whole as she wished it would, so she cleared her throat and made an attempt at sounding business-like. "So Mr. Miyagi, does this conclude our lesson? Should I come back at the same time tomorrow?"

He paused and appeared to think it over. "I don't think so. No."

"No?" she asked, hating the note of distress in her voice.

"No," he said again. "For our next lesson I'd like to go on a field trip."

"A field trip?" Why was she repeating everything he said?

"Yes." He nodded. "If you're up for it."

"Where?" Knowing Brock, it could be anywhere. She wanted to be at least somewhat prepared for whatever he had in store.

Brock leaned against the workbench and crossed his feet at the ankles. "How would Mr. Miyagi answer that question?"

Anya narrowed her gaze. "You're not going to tell me, are you?"

He smirked, clearly satisfied with himself. "Nope."

Impossible. The man was impossible.

Brock stomped his feet to loosen the snow from his boots as he stepped inside the ski patrol headquarters the next morning. The snow had finally stopped falling, at least for the time being. But it still clung to the ground—and everything else in Alaska, it seemed—as it would until the summer sun came and finally melted it all away. According to his research, Aurora was under snowfall nine months out of the year.

That meant nine months of danger of a slide. Slopes with an underlayer of old snow made things even worse. Aurora had snow in abundance. Weak snow. New snow. All kinds of snow.

"Good morning. Who's your friend?" Cole's eyebrows rose as he looked up from the book he was reading and took in the sight of Brock.

Brock loosened his arms from his backpack and let it slide gently to the floor. Aspen's copper-colored head poked out from the top. He let out a little woof, indicating he was more than ready to be let loose.

"Morning. This is Aspen. He's one of the pups in training I told you about." Brock unzipped the backpack, and Aspen wiggled his way out.

"Why are you carrying him around like that? He looks more than capable of tromping through the snow." Cole whistled for the dog and gave him a good scratch behind the ears. Aspen yelped with glee.

The two of them were bonding already. Good. "Sometimes the dogs need to be carried on the mountain—when loading onto a ski lift or riding a snow machine, for instance. I get in practice for those skills when I can."

"I see." Cole nodded and closed the book he'd been reading. Small. Black leather. Brock recognized it at once as a Bible. "He's a good size for that, I suppose."

"That's one of the reasons I use this breed—the Nova Scotia Duck Tolling Retriever. They're trainable and sturdy, yet compact enough to make convenient search dogs." Brock hung his backpack on a hook by the door to the cabin and sank into a chair at the table opposite Cole.

"How long have you had him?"

"Since he was eight weeks old. His littermate too—Sherlock. He's not quite ready to start training up here." But he would be soon, if the way he was responding to Anya was any indication. "I have a breeder in Washington who I work with to select pups that look like good candidates for search and rescue dogs."

"That must be hard." With Aspen flopped belly-up at his feet, Cole poured Brock a cup of coffee from the box in the center of the table and slid it toward him.

As soon as he took the first sip, Brock knew it was from Anya's coffee bar. It was far too good to come from anywhere else. He was beginning to understand why the Northern Lights Inn was such a draw. "What's hard?"

Cole shrugged and nudged Aspen with his foot. "Training the dogs as pups and then leaving them behind."

"I suppose." Brock frowned. He'd never thought of it as leaving the dogs behind. Sure, it was hard sometimes. He spent almost every waking hour with the pups. Forming attachments was unavoidable. But it was his job, what he did best—train the search dogs and put them to work in the places where they were most needed.

"Well, don't you worry. We'll take great care of this little fella." Cole bent and rubbed Aspen's belly, sending the pup into throes of delight. "And the other one too."

"Sherlock," Brock said absently, still slightly thrown by the notion of leaving the dogs behind. He hoped the Tollers didn't think of it that way. "The other one's name is Sherlock."

He took another sip of his coffee. Maybe a healthy dose of caffeine would clear his head. The last thing he needed was to go soft. It wasn't as if he were abandoning the dogs. He was putting them to work. They were helping people. *He* was helping people.

Cole rose from his chair and shrugged into his parka. "Oh, by the way, I signed you up for the Reindeer Run."

The sudden change of subject threw Brock for a moment. *Reindeer Run?* Then he remembered Anya's cute little smirk. *You should do it. Actually now that I think about it, the Reindeer Run is right up your alley.*

"You signed me up?" he asked, still trying the shake the image of that wry smile. Of those eyes…

"Yep. The ski patrol enters the race every year as a team. It'll be fun." Cole zipped up his jacket as he reached for the door. "I'm headed out to gas up the snow machine. We'll meet back here in an hour or so for training, right?"

"Right." Brock nodded.

Aspen sat up and swiveled his head back and forth

between the two of them as if asking whether or not he should follow Cole.

"You're with me, Aspen," Brock said.

For now anyway.

The dog scuttled over to him and rested his chin on Brock's knee. Cole shut the door behind him, and Brock sighed.

He laid his hand on Aspen's head. "You get it, right? This is your home now."

Aspen swiped Brock's hand with his tongue.

"Good boy." Brock ran the pad of his thumb over the dog's head in lazy circles.

Of course the dog understood. And if he didn't, he would. He was a dog, after all. He'd bond with whoever spent time with him and fed him every day. By this time next year, Brock would be a distant memory to both Aspen and Sherlock. It was straightforward with animals. At least that's what Brock always told himself, making it all the more easy for him to walk away.

With people, however, things were rarely so simple. Which was precisely why Brock didn't let himself get close—to anyone. It was also why he didn't like the sound of the Reindeer Run.

He wasn't here to put down roots, so he saw no point in getting involved in community events. And a team event? It sounded even more problematic. The guys on the ski patrol didn't need to start thinking of him as part of their team. But Cole had already signed him up, so he didn't really have a choice in the matter.

Maybe it wouldn't be so bad. What could be the harm in running five kilometers—or whatever the Reindeer Run involved—with the guys? It couldn't be any more dangerous than spending every evening with Anya.

Anya.

Something moved in Brock's chest at the thought of her. Something warm, intangible and most definitely not invited.

Convinced he was imagining things, he scolded himself. The thing with Anya was nothing. He was helping her out, that's all. And, likewise, she was helping him with the pups. Wax on, wax off, just like she'd said. He wasn't doing anything wrong.

His throat suddenly grew tight, and his gaze was drawn to Cole's Bible sitting in the center of the table.

In Brock's experience, it wasn't unusual to find a Bible in a ski patrol headquarters. When the business at hand involved saving people's lives, faith in a higher power never hurt. And Brock had always been a believer himself. It had just been a while since he'd picked up the good book. A long while.

He reached for the Bible. The sheer weight of it felt comforting in his hands. The edges of the supple, leather cover were tattered and worn from what looked like years of use. Brock's own Bible looked a fair bit newer and was packed up in one of the boxes back at the house. At least he thought it was. The boxes followed him from one place to the next, but sometimes he didn't even bother to unpack them. What was the point?

He flipped the book open and was relieved when his fingers automatically found the page and verse he was searching for—Luke 19:10.

For the Son of Man came to seek and to save what was lost.

It was the verse he'd based his life on.

Brock certainly didn't have a savior complex. He knew all too well he was a man, full of more than his share of flaws. He'd never felt comfortable with the label *hero* no matter how many times it was applied to him.

But he'd always considered what he did to be a calling—finding those who'd been swallowed up by the snow, and teaching others to do the same. His parents, particularly his mother, worried over him and his *obsession,* as they called it. Was it an obsession? Maybe. Brock had devoted his life to it, to the exclusion of everything else.

And every*one* else.

It demanded everything from him, and he was freely willing to give it. The thought of sharing his life with someone, of loving someone, only filled him with dread. Without warning, people vanished. Even loved ones. He knew that only too well.

But that was okay because without his calling, the disappearance of his brother would have been for nothing. And that would have been unacceptable. At least he'd made something meaningful out of all that pain.

For the Son of Man came to seek and to save what was lost.

He was doing God's work. No one would be hurt by it. Not him, not Anya and certainly not the dogs.

At least that's what he told himself as he closed the Bible and pushed it away, out of arm's reach.

Chapter Five

"Hi Mom, it's me." Anya followed the whirring sound of her mother's sewing machine through the darkened living room of her childhood home, down the hall and to the sewing room.

The sewing room, formerly Anya's bedroom, was where her mother could most often be found, bent over the Singer, stitching together brightly colored suedes, velvets and sometimes even furs. Today, like most other days, an array of traditional Inuit anoraks and parkas hung across the length of the curtain rod. Some were complete, ready to be shipped off to the native arts cooperative gallery in Anchorage, where her mother's work was sold. Others still needed finishing touches here and there. But they were all beautiful, even in their various stages of completion. Beautiful and one of a kind.

"Hello, sweetheart." Her mother glanced up from the machine but kept feeding fabric toward the needle. "Give me just a minute. I'm almost finished with this sleeve."

"Sure." Anya sat on the foot of the bed—the same twin mattress she'd slept on from first through twelfth grade—and watched.

As always, her gaze was drawn toward her mother's hair, twisted into a thick braid that ran down the middle of her back. When she was a girl, Anya had wanted nothing more than to look like her mother. Or any of the other women in her family, really. They all had warm mocha skin, dark, mysterious eyes and long hair as black and shiny as raven's wings. Anya's mother may have only been part Inuit, but she looked every inch a native Alaskan, as did her aunts and cousins.

Anya's appearance couldn't have been more different. With her gangly limbs, ivory complexion and ribbon of chestnut hair, which glowed almost amber in the sunshine, she resembled a tourist from the Lower 48 more than any of the native Alaskan children in her classes at school. But it was her eyes that really set her apart.

Who had violet eyes?

No one Anya had ever seen, other than the strange-looking girl she saw in the mirror every day. As if her name wasn't awful enough: Anya Petrova. A fleeting glance at her mother was sufficient to tell anyone who wondered about such things that the Russian name was solely her father's doing.

eed any help from your church, Anya. I
re of my own roof." Her mother turned
d the sewing machine, her wrist flicking
hile she wound the bobbin.

let them come help. They want to do this."
what? What happens after they deice my
ey'll expect me to show up at church, that's

, they won't." *And even if they did, would that
be so bad?* "It's not like that, Mom. No one
expect anything of you in return. They're just
people who want to help."

er back may have been turned, but Anya could
se her mother's skeptical eye roll, could feel the
terness behind it.

Anya rested a hand on her shoulder. "*I* want to
elp. Please let me take care of this for you."

Her mother stiffened, saying nothing, and the
sewing machine purred to life once again.

Anya would have preferred a spoken agreement,
but she figured this was as close as she was going to
get. Before her mother had a change of heart, Anya
gave her shoulder a final pat, then slipped from her
old bedroom and back out into the snow.

"Where are we going again?" Anya asked as she
climbed onto the passenger seat of Brock's truck.

"Nice try." He cast her a quick glance as she
got settled. Then he closed the passenger door and

Like most girls, all she'd wanted was to fit in, to
be like everyone else. But she wasn't like everyone
else, not even her own mother. The differences between them were written all over Anya's face.

"What brings you by, Anya?" The sewing machine slowed to a stop. Anya's mother took her foot
off the pedal and swiveled to face the bed.

Anya shrugged. "I just wanted to stop by and visit
for a minute. I can't stay long, though."

She didn't get into the reason why—Brock's field
trip. Because it was a nonevent as far as she was
concerned. Not worth mentioning.

*Then why is just the thought of it making me ner-
vous enough to break into a sweat?*

She shrugged out of her parka. "It's warm in
here."

"Is it?" Her mother frowned and glanced at the
window, completely obscured by the parkas hanging
from the rod. "It's snowing again, right?"

"Yes, it's really coming down. I brought you a
coffee." Anya thrust a cup toward her. "An Almond
Joy latte. Today's special."

She took the cup and gave the tiny hole in its plastic lid a wary sniff. "You know I can't sleep when
I drink this stuff."

"It's decaf, Mom."

"Okay." She took a dainty sip. "Mmm. This is
really good."

Anya smiled a relieved smile. She hadn't actually

stopped by for a simple visit. The flavored coffee was the buffer—bribe had a rather ugly ring to it—she hoped would help her mother accept the news she had to share.

She took a deep breath and prepared herself to spit it out, to just say it. Time was ticking, and Brock would be at her cottage in less than an hour. "A group of people at my church is getting together for a local outreach project in a couple weeks."

"Oh?" Her mother's mouth turned down in a slight frown.

Not a good sign. Anya plowed on anyway. "I signed us up."

"What does that mean? You've signed us up to do chores for people? With your *church*?" Her mother couldn't have looked more horrified.

If Anya had once been uncomfortable with the notion of God, her mother's resistance could only be described as Alaskan-sized in its scope. After Anya had first heard those words—*never will I leave you*—she recounted them earnestly to her mother, struggling to explain how it had felt like God Himself had dropped down from the rafters of the sanctuary and whispered them in her ear. Her newfound faith had been a source of mystery to her mother. She was still reeling from the desertion of her husband, even after twenty-six years. The idea of a faithful God was too foreign for her to comprehend.

Anya sat up a little straighter, wishing they

weren't having this c̶ ̶ ̶ ̶ room. Sitting on the na̶ ̶ like a five year old instea̶ ̶ I put our names on the lis̶ with certain projects. I was ̶ roof. There's a good four i̶ ̶ Mom. All that weight can't be ̶

"My house. Not *the* house. Yo̶ in six years. So when you say y̶ on the list, you really mean *my* na̶

"Sort of," Anya said under her b̶ want to get technical about it."

Although if things didn't change with ̶ she might be living in this small room o̶ Moving back home wasn't exactly an ideal ̶ but where else could she go?

Anya wasn't about to admit that the out̶ project was designed mainly to help the widow̶ Aurora. A technicality, in her opinion. Her moth̶ might as well have been a widow. Actually, thoug̶ Anya hated to admit it, she could already be a widow.

She hadn't considered the idea before, even when she'd written her mother's name and address on the list. But there was no guarantee her father was still alive, wherever he was. Anya blinked and waited for a wave of grief to wash over her at the prospect. The wave never came. Instead she felt a familiar, icy numbness in her chest.

jogged through the snow to the driver's side, pausing on the way to check on Sherlock and Aspen situated in their crates in the back.

"We're going on a field trip," he said again as he settled himself beside her and cranked the ignition to life.

"That doesn't really answer my question." Anya couldn't help but grin despite Brock's refusal to be more specific.

He'd worn another crazy hat. Instead of antlers, this one sported pointy wolf ears and a comically long toothy muzzle that stuck out over his head. He looked utterly ridiculous. Why Anya found it charming was a mystery she would never understand.

"You look like a caricature of the Big Bad Wolf. Should I have worn my red hoodie?"

"You look fine." He cracked one of his rare smiles.

Anya's stomach fluttered, and she looked away. "So I shouldn't expect to see anyone else in costume?"

"It's a socialization tool, not a costume," he said dryly.

Anya snorted. "Keep telling yourself that."

Brock's response was little more than an amused grunt and a shake of his head. He said nothing and kept his eyes glued on the road.

For that, Anya was grateful. On the rare moments he locked his icy-blue eyes on hers, she went all soft inside.

It was annoying. But she really couldn't help it. She was only human. She might have had her heart broken a time or two, but she could still recognize a handsome man when she saw one. And Brock certainly fit the bill in that regard. That strong jaw and those cheekbones would have looked more appropriate on a marble sculpture in an art museum somewhere than they did in Aurora, Alaska. Not that she was complaining...

She scooted farther away from him on the bench seat of the truck and put an extra inch or two of space between them. It wasn't much, but it couldn't hurt.

It was then that she refocused her attention on the road and realized where they were headed.

She frowned. "Are we going up to the ski mountain?"

"Yep." He nodded at the familiar wooden sign nestled among a cluster of evergreens on the side of the road advertising the entrance to Aurora Ski Resort.

Great.

She hadn't been up on the mountain since the day of Speed's infamous interview.

"Is that okay?" Brock asked, cruising past the sign and unknowingly toward the scene of her humiliation.

A lump lodged in her throat. She did her best to swallow it. "Sure. I thought you were giving me another dog training lesson, that's all. That *is* why I show up at your house every afternoon."

Her words came out with a little more bite than she'd planned. Brock either didn't notice, or he didn't care. He slid the truck into a parking place and unclicked his seatbelt. "Patience, grasshopper."

She sighed and let herself out of the truck before he could come around and open her door for her. This wasn't a date, after all. And it was beginning to look less and less like a dog training class. Not that her previous lessons had been all that conventional. But still. She would have liked to know exactly what they were doing here. She wasn't altogether thrilled to be back on the mountain, but she was undoubtedly intrigued.

Brock made quick work of unloading Sherlock and Aspen from their crates. Once free, Aspen sat calmly and professionally at Brock's feet awaiting a command. Sherlock, however, bounded straight toward Anya.

"Good boy," she cooed and scratched Sherlock behind his ears.

Sherlock wagged his tail, sending snow flying in all directions.

Brock shook his head and stepped out of the way. "He's developing a crush on you, you know."

Anya straightened. "What?"

"Sherlock." Brock pinned the dog with a stern look. "He's falling for you."

So she couldn't manage to get a man to stick around, but a dog was in love with her? "Be still my heart."

"I'm serious," he said. If he thought she could take a single word he said seriously while he was wearing that hat, he was kidding himself.

She shrugged. "He likes me."

"So long as he keeps his focus…"

She gave Sherlock a kiss on the head. "You will, won't you, boy?"

The dog writhed with delight.

Brock shook his head. "Told you." And he strode off in the other direction.

Anya fell in step beside him, the deep snow gobbling up her footsteps as they went. She'd expected him to lead her to the ski patrol cabin, but once it came into view he bypassed the front door and walked instead to an outer building. Like the patrol headquarters, it was fashioned to resemble a log cabin, only smaller.

Brock pulled on the building's wide double door, and it opened with a creak. Two snowmobiles—both candy-apple red and adorned with the ski patrol's signature white cross—sat side by side.

Anya raised her brows. "Are we going for a ride?"

"The dogs are. Their inaugural ride, actually. Do you know how to drive one of these things?" He eyed the snow machines.

"Are you kidding? I could drive one of these

before I ever got behind the wheel of a car." Of course, it had been years since she'd driven one—she hadn't come within ten feet of a snow machine since the days when she used to accompany Speed to the ski mountain—but Brock didn't need to know that. It wasn't as though she'd forgotten how. It was like riding a bicycle, wasn't it? A very fast, very powerful bicycle.

"Excellent. That's what I like to hear." Brock smiled and looked directly at her for the briefest of moments. Her toes, still buried under inches of snow, began to thaw slightly. "Hop on."

She did as he asked, settling herself on one of the smooth leather seats. She had no clue where she was supposed to put a dog, but Brock soon solved that dilemma by having Sherlock sit directly in front of her. Then he took her hands and placed them on the handlebars, effectively caging Sherlock in.

Brock walked a few feet backward and narrowed his gaze at them. "Comfortable?"

"Sure." It was a nice machine. Far nicer than any of the others she'd driven. Having Sherlock nestled against her somehow made her relax too. He smelled like puppy. That was always a good thing.

"Sherlock looks pretty happy up there." Brock smirked.

"He should. He's in love with me. Remember?"

Brock just shook his head, peeled off the ridiculous wolf hat and climbed onto the other snowmobile.

Once Aspen was in place, Brock revved his machine to life and gave Anya the signal to do the same. Then she followed him out of the little log building and onto the trail.

All the while she could hear Brock murmuring soothing words of encouragement to Aspen, even over the hum of the engines. Although the reassurance was clearly not meant for her, Anya felt buoyed by it. Soon, memories of being on these same slopes, riding alongside Speed up to the "sweet spot" as he'd always called it—the piste, where he could really let loose on his skis—faded. With the wind whipping against her face, blowing and lifting Sherlock's copper-colored ears until they looked as though they were floating, Anya began to feel alive. Alive in a way she hadn't felt for a very long time.

When it was clear Sherlock was enjoying the ride every bit as much as she was, Anya pushed her thumb against the throttle and upped her speed. Soon, she'd passed Brock and instead of riding side by side, he was following her along the tree-lined path of packed snow. At the end of the trail, she pulled her machine to a stop and waited for Brock and Aspen to catch up.

"Good boy, Sherlock. That was fun, huh?"

The dog swiped her face with his tongue. She laughed and smoothed down her hair. She was sure she looked like a mess—her eyes stung and watered from the bite of arctic air, and her cheeks felt chapped, burned by the wind. Sure enough, though, when Brock pulled his snowmobile alongside hers, he looked like he'd ridden straight off the cover of an adventure magazine. Rugged and disheveled just to the point of wildness, causing her to feel suddenly off-kilter.

It was unnerving.

So she decided a punishment was in order. She leaned forward and shook the peeling trunk of a slender pine tree until one of its low-lying branches dumped a pile of snow directly on Brock's head.

"Hey," he shouted.

A deep, throaty laugh rose up from her lungs, raw from the rush of Alaskan air.

"You're not afraid of much, are you?" He raked a gloved hand through his hair, now wet with slush.

On the contrary, she thought. *You scare me, Brock Parker. You scare me very much.*

"No." She lifted her chin, but his gaze was focused on the center of her forehead. Again. "While that was loads of fun, and obviously helpful for the avalanche dogs, how exactly does playing around on snow machines help Dolce?"

"It doesn't." Before she could protest, he pulled something from the pocket of his parka—a toy that resembled three rubber balls stacked one on top of the other. It was as red as the snow mobiles and topped with a shiny bow. "But this does."

He tossed it to her. She caught it and turned it

over in her hand, inspecting it. She chose to ignore the bow, not even wanting to venture a guess what it meant. "What is this?"

"It's a training tool. See the hole in the top?"

Sure enough, there was a hole about the size of a quarter on the top of the toy. She peered inside and saw nothing. "Yes?"

"Next time you need to leave the house and Dolce is there unattended, fill that thing up with treats. Then seal the hole with a good dollop of peanut butter."

"Peanut butter?" She lifted a brow.

"I guarantee it will keep her quiet." He shrugged. "You could even hide it somewhere for her to find. That would keep her busy even longer. But start out with an easy spot."

"Okay." She looked down at the red toy again, topped with the pretty bow, and grew suddenly bashful. "This is very sweet of you. Thank you."

Brock cleared his throat and looked at an insignificant spot on the snowy ground. He suddenly appeared as self-conscious as a man who wore such ridiculous get-ups possibly could. "You're welcome."

Neither one of them said a word for a prolonged, awkward moment. Finally, Brock lifted his gaze to her again. "There's something I want to ask you."

Anya's hands began to shake. She buried them in Sherlock's soft fur. "Okay."

"I was wondering if you'd like to make this a

regular thing…helping me train the avalanche dogs up here on the mountain. Cole and the others are stretched to their limit, and frankly, I could use another pair of hands. You obviously have a knack for it." He glanced at Sherlock and then back at Anya. "What do you think?"

Anya didn't need to think about it at all. It was a terrible idea. Things were already confusing enough without spending even more time with Brock than absolutely necessary.

She would just say no. Plain and simple.

"Yes." The word slipped right out of her rebellious mouth. "I'd love to."

"Great. Care to race back?" Brock gave her a quick wink, a simple gesture that was the physical embodiment of all the reasons this new arrangement was a bad idea. Or maybe the way it made her stomach flutter was the actual reason.

Either way, Anya was grateful for the opportunity to zip away from him. "You're on."

Chapter Six

"Remind me why we're doing this again." Anya slipped off her hiking boots and wiggled her sock feet. "It's winter. In Alaska. Our toes won't see the light of day for months."

Sue let out a sigh as she dipped her feet in the small tub of bubbly water attached to the chair where she sat between Anya and Clementine. "Just obey Clementine's orders. This feels divine."

"I told you," Clementine said in a singsong voice. "Who needs a reason for pedicures?"

"Exactly. In fact, right now I'm wondering why we don't do this more often." Sue leaned back and closed her eyes.

The three of them were lined up, side by side, in plush leather chairs at Aurora's one and only nail salon, *North Pole Nails*. Anya couldn't quite figure out where the name had come from because it wasn't exactly geographically accurate. Sure, it snowed in

Aurora more often than not. A lot more often. And there was an abundance of reindeer in and around the area. But the town wasn't even inside the Arctic Circle, much less at the North Pole.

None of that mattered once Anya's feet were immersed in hot, soapy water. Santa Claus could have walked right through the door and she'd scarcely have noticed.

"Oh my. This is nice. Very nice." Anya leaned back against the soft leather and allowed herself to relax. As the bubbles danced against her toes, the part of her brain that constantly wondered what Dolce was doing in her absence even seemed to let out a sigh.

The nail technician smiled and dropped a scoop of what looked like bath salts in the water.

"Mmm. What's that scent?" Sue asked. "It smells fantastic."

"Frosted Snowflake," the nail tech said. "It's our most popular scent."

Again, a mistake. Anya was certain snow didn't have a scent. Nor did frost, for that matter. But who cared? Her toes were warm and toasty, and in a minute, someone would be massaging her feet.

"I've been trying to get you two to come do this for weeks now," Clementine said.

Sue laughed. "Don't worry. Next time, just say the word and we'll be here. Right, Anya?"

"Right." Anya nodded. "Although my schedule is getting crazier by the day."

Clementine looked up from the magazine she'd brought along—*Nature World.* Before moving to Alaska, Clementine worked for the slick publication as a photo researcher. Nowadays, she liked to flip through it and show them the photographs her friend and former coworker, Natalie, had selected to accompany the articles. "What do you mean? Are you working extra hours at the coffee bar?"

"No." Anya felt lightheaded all of a sudden. Silly, really. She attributed it to the bubbly footbath. "Brock has asked me to help him train the new avalanche search dogs. We took them out on snowmobiles yesterday."

"Wow, that sounds…interesting." Clementine lifted a brow. "Snowmobiling together? It wasn't a date, was it?"

"Hardly." Then why were her cheeks growing so warm just thinking about it? "Ben didn't bring dogs along on your first date, did he?"

"Actually, he did. A dozen or so of them. We went dog sledding."

Sue laughed. "Ahh, the life of a musher's wife. I can relate."

For some reason, Anya's chest felt hollow while she listened to Sue and Clementine talk about their husbands. "I repeat—it wasn't a date."

Clementine and Sue exchanged loaded glances. Anya ignored them.

Clementine cleared her throat. "What exactly will you be doing with the avalanche dogs?"

"I'm not sure. Brock isn't what I'd call forthcoming with information." That was possibly the understatement of the century. "All I managed to get out of him was that tomorrow I'll be hiding in a trench so the dogs can practice finding me."

"Where?" Sue asked.

"Up on the mountain." Anya nodded toward the window. Its frame perfectly showcased the snow-capped mountains of the ski resort.

Pretty as a picture, Anya mused.

That was odd. She hadn't thought of the ski mountain with anything but dread in a long time. As much as she hated to admit it, she supposed Brock was to thank for her new attitude.

"Being buried alive in the snow? On a mountain?" Sue's brow furrowed. "Won't that be dangerous?"

Anya shrugged. "I don't know. I haven't actually thought about it. I really enjoy working with the dogs, though. It's fun, and I feel like I'm doing something important."

"That's great. I'm happy for you." Clementine lifted her feet from the sudsy water, and the nail tech patted them dry.

"Just be careful." Sue reached over and gave her arm a squeeze. "Please."

"I will. I promise." Anya closed her eyes again and burrowed into the comfy chair.

She wondered why she hadn't given any thought to the dangers of working on the mountain. In a typical week, dozens of people were injured up there. That's why the ski patrol was so important.

The mountain didn't scare Anya, though. Some things just seemed far more perilous than snow, wind and jagged peaks.

Unfortunately for her, Brock Parker was at the tip-top of that list.

Brock didn't like the looks of the weather. There was something about the sky—that odd shade of dove gray with hints of mossy green. It resembled a bruise, as if the sky had taken a good pummeling and was biding its time until it healed, readying itself to unleash a torrent of retribution.

"Something wrong?" Cole stomped toward him through the inches of fresh powder the storm had dumped on them the night before.

Brock shook his head but kept his mouth shut. Now wasn't the time to bring up his thoughts of impending trouble. Three people were scheduled to join them any minute for the ski patrol's first avalanche drill. As gray as the sky might appear, it wasn't altogether out of the ordinary. His apprehension wasn't rooted in any real, physical threat. It was more of a feeling, a certain intuition he'd honed over the years. Besides, they were already doing anything and everything that could be done to make the mountain safe. Ideally, today's training would be the beginning of regularly scheduled avalanche drills that would continue long after Brock had gone. But the ski patrol was clearly spread pretty thin, and Cole had yet to make a decision about who would be in charge of the program once Brock got it up and running. From what Brock had seen, none of the other members of the patrol had the time required to really make the program a success.

He ran his fingers over the top of Sherlock's soft red fur. The dog's tail beat happily against Brock's leg, taking the edge off his worry. He couldn't micromanage Aurora's ski patrol. That wasn't his job. It was Cole's. Brock didn't know why he'd begun to lose sleep over what would happen on the mountain once he'd gone. He usually didn't have this problem.

Sherlock's tail wagged with even greater enthusiasm, prompting Brock to look up. Anya approached them, dressed in a fur-trimmed parka and a knit hat that was nearly as red as her cheeks.

"Good morning," she said, rather crisply, when she reached him.

She was all business.

Until Sherlock bounded to her side.

Then she dropped to her knees right there in the snow and rubbed Sherlock from head to tail in a frenzy-inducing fit of affection. The dog gave her a gleeful swipe of his tongue, and she threw her head back and laughed.

The set of Brock's jaw hardened involuntarily, and with horror he realized he was jealous. Jealous of a dog.

It was ludicrous.

Yet the truth of it settled in his gut.

"Shall we get started?" he asked, an edge creeping into his voice.

Anya straightened. "Sure. What would you like me to do, boss?"

Boss?

"I'm not your boss," he said. Didn't she realize how much he needed her help? Maybe not. It wasn't as if he'd told her so. "We're in this together, you know. We're a team. All of us."

"Of course." Her voice softened a bit. "Thank you again, by the way, for the rubber toy. Dolce was quiet as a mouse when I left the house just now."

"Good." Brock warmed with pleasure. Pleasure inordinately out of proportion to the situation. He'd given her a dog toy, not a diamond. What was wrong with him?

He shook off the feeling. What did diamonds have to do with avalanche training anyway? He was losing it. "Here come the others. Luke and Jackson have been busy digging trenches for our exercise."

"For hiding?"

"Yes, for hiding. It's the first step in getting the

dogs acclimated to the idea of searching." He paused while Luke and Jackson waded through the snow to join them. Aspen bounded alongside Jackson, and just like Sherlock, his tail began to wag when he spotted Anya.

The difference was that anyone and everyone made Aspen's tail wag. Sherlock, however, only had eyes for Anya. It was beginning to pose a problem. Not that he could do anything about it right now. They had work to do.

Brock began to introduce Anya to Cole, Luke and Jackson, but with Aurora being such a tight-knit community, they all knew one another already. "Okay then, time to get started. Today we're going to have the dogs work to find their own handlers. In the beginning, it's best to have them search for someone they already know and love."

He pointed a gloved hand at Jackson and Aspen. "Jackson, you've been assigned to work with Aspen, right?"

"Yep."

Brock turned to Cole. "Who've you picked as a handler for Sherlock?"

"No one." Cole shrugged. "We're short-handed. I can't really afford to put another member of the patrol with a dog full time."

Brock's temples throbbed. There it was again—that tug of worry about what would happen here after he'd gone. Against his better judgment, he ventured a glance in Anya's direction. The nagging pain in his head only intensified. He didn't want to believe she was the reason he cared so much about Aurora. But there it was—the truth looking right back at him with striking violet eyes.

Someone cleared his throat. Brock tore his gaze from Anya and realized it was Cole.

"What about Anya?" Cole asked, jerking his head toward her. "The dog certainly seems to like her."

Indeed, Sherlock was on his back writhing in ecstasy at Anya's feet, sending snow flying in every direction.

Brock shook his head. All that hand-feeding and reading aloud had created a bit of a monster. Sherlock's doggy crush aside, Anya acting as his handler wasn't the best idea. The dog needed to start bonding with whoever would act as his permanent partner. That, of course, was a problem, because he didn't have a permanent partner yet.

"All right," Brock said. "Anya will work with Sherlock."

The dog leapt to his feet and leaned against her legs in a posture that clearly said *Mine*. Once again, Brock found himself fighting off an uncomfortable sensation he didn't want to admit was jealousy.

"Let's begin," he said, wishing desperately that he could focus solely on the task at hand. He pulled two knotted rope toys from his pockets and tossed one to Anya and the other to Jackson. "These will be the rewards for the dogs when they find you. Once you've been located, offer your dog loads of praise and play tug of war with them for a few seconds. We want the experience to be as positive and fun as possible for them."

"Then shouldn't we offer them food or treats instead of just praise?" Jackson asked.

Brock shook his head. "No. Good question, though. We don't train with food because we're teaching the dogs to search for human scent—the scent of survivors buried under the snow pack. If we train with food, the dogs will become conditioned to search for the scent of treats instead of victims."

Cole nodded. "That makes sense."

"The favored reward for search and rescue work is play and praise. Lots of it." Brock aimed his gaze at Jackson and Anya. "When your dog finds you, be enthusiastic. Throw an all-out party. Got it?"

"Got it," Jackson said.

Anya nodded, grinning from ear to ear. Brock had never seen anyone so excited about the idea of hiding in a snow trench. He'd known she'd be the right choice to help with training. Her enthusiasm mirrored his own passion for search work. Seeing her in action brought out the teacher in him, and it was almost enough to make him forget about the color of her eyes.

Emphasis on *almost*.

He pointed to Cole and Luke. "Okay, you two are

going to hold onto the dogs while Anya and Jackson hide."

Brock showed them each how to grasp Aspen and Sherlock's collars with an underhand grip and instructed them to hang on tight.

"We're going to do this one at a time. Anya, you're up first. You ready?" he asked.

"I sure am." The wind whipped between them, sending the hair that tumbled down her back flying in all directions. Brock had to stop himself from reaching out and sweeping a lock of it from her eyes.

He jammed his hands in his pockets. Just in case. "I want you to shower some affection on Sherlock. Get him good and excited. Make him go bonkers. Then tell him to come find you before you head for the trench."

"Now?"

"Yup." He took a step out of the way.

Then there was little to do but watch as she did exactly as he said. It didn't take much for her to get Sherlock excited about the search. She gave him a good scratch behind the ears, and he immediately started tugging against Cole's grip, lunging and bouncing on his hind legs in an attempt to get to her. By the time she started asking him if he wanted to come find her, Sherlock looked as though he might jerk Cole's arm right out of its socket.

Brock watched Anya run up the hill, her feet sinking deeper in the snow with each step. Sherlock's barks grew louder and more urgent, bouncing off the surrounding evergreens when Anya disappeared into the trench.

Brock gave her a few seconds to get settled before he gave Cole a silent signal to release Sherlock. Once free, the dog made a beeline for the deep burrow in the snow where Anya waited to be found. Even though it was a good thirty feet away, Brock could hear her praising Sherlock and telling him what a good boy he was, loud and clear from inside the confines of the snowy trough.

Cole's eyebrows rose in obvious surprise. "Wow. That was impressive."

"Yes." Brock nodded thoughtfully. "Yes, it was."

His throat grew scratchy, and he blinked hard against the snow flurries hitting his eyes. The swell of pride that hit him square in the chest took him by surprise. Although its cause did not.

She was a natural, as he'd thought she would be.

He just hoped Sherlock would work as hard to find a real victim.

The next morning Anya did something she'd never done before. Just a day after her triumphant training session with Sherlock, Anya Petrova— barista extraordinaire—burned the coffee.

What in the world?

She stared into the pot of Alaska Klondike Roast

and winced at the brown sludge stuck to the bottom, wondering how it had happened.

"What's that smell?" Zoey asked as she leaned over Anya's shoulder and peered at the coffeepot.

Anya hadn't even taken note of her arrival. Was her head that far up in the clouds?

Apparently so.

"Nothing." She plunged the coffeepot under the faucet and flipped on the hot water before Zoey could see the mess she'd made.

Too late. "I never thought I'd see the day you burned the coffee." Zoey shook her head in disbelief.

Anya could hardly blame her. She couldn't believe it either. "I'm sorry."

Zoey frowned. "Why are you apologizing? You're the boss around here. Remember?"

She sighed. "I suppose I am."

Zoey reached around her to squirt some soap in the coffeepot, then gave her arm a comforting squeeze. "Don't beat yourself up about it. We all make mistakes."

"Never before." She shook her head. "Not here."

Making coffee was her thing. She'd always been great at it. Not that it was all that difficult, but still. Zoey went to work scrubbing the pot for her, which made her feel even worse.

"You've been somewhat distracted lately." Zoey's tone was far from accusatory. She sounded concerned more than anything, with a dash of affection thrown in for good measure.

Anya pulled a face. "Is it that obvious?"

"Pretty much." Zoey smiled. "I think I know what it is."

Inexplicably, Brock's face flashed in Anya's mind. "You do?"

"Yes." Zoey nodded. "It's the work you're doing with the ski patrol, isn't it? All that time you're spending training the dogs?"

"That might have something to do with it." Anya bit her lip. It was true. She'd been spending an awful lot of time up on the mountain. And when she wasn't working with the dogs, she was thinking about them. She couldn't help it. The work she was doing with the search and rescue unit filled her with a sense of purpose she'd never found at the coffee bar.

"You love it. I can see it whenever you talk about it. You just light up from the inside." Zoey paused from scrubbing the pot and glanced up at her. "Hey, don't look so worried. It's only a little burned coffee. There's nothing to be afraid of."

"Nothing to be afraid of," Anya repeated.

She didn't believe a word of it. There was quite a lot to be afraid of, actually.

Anya wouldn't have believed it possible, but Brock's presence in Aurora had grown even more problematic. In addition to dealing with the conflicting feelings she'd been battling since the moment he'd removed that nutty bear head, now he'd shown her a whole new world she hadn't even known existed. He'd given her the chance to do something with her life. Something real. Something of value. She hadn't realized just how much she'd needed to feel used by God until Sherlock had bounded toward her hiding place, his victory barks bouncing off the evergreens.

Maybe someday he would save someone's life. And she would have been a part of that. A small part, obviously, but the idea of it sent a shiver up her spine.

How would she ever go back to the way things were before?

She swallowed and tried not to think about what would happen when Brock left, whether she would ever stand atop that mountain again, or if she would spend the rest of her life making coffee.

Or burning coffee, as the case may be.

"Here comes your hero." Zoey nodded to the circular door at the hotel entrance.

Sure enough, Brock was spinning his way inside the circular door, his shoulders so broad they nearly filled the door frame. "Please don't call him that." *Your hero.* "Please."

"Whatever you say." Zoey shrugged and pulled a book from one of the shelves under the counter.

Anya stared at the cover. "*Principles of Aviation?* A little light reading?"

"Something like that," Zoey mumbled, her eyes widening with joy as she flipped to a page featuring a diagram of a flight deck.

Perhaps Anya wasn't the only one who dreamed of greater things. The thought brought Anya some comfort, even though the aroma of burned coffee beans still lingered.

"Good morning." Brock paused, halfway perched on one of the stools across the counter. He sniffed. "What's that smell?"

Zoey raised her head from her airplane diagram. "I don't smell anything." She winked at Anya.

Brock's gaze darted between the two of them. "Then I guess I'll have a cup of coffee."

"Coming right up." Anya poured a cup from the batch she'd managed not to burn and slid the mug toward Brock.

He eyed it warily before taking a sip. Then he sat the mug back down and stared into the coffee. Naturally. Anywhere but directly at her. "I wanted to come by and tell you what a great job you did yesterday."

"Oh. Wow." For Brock, it was nothing short of effusive. Anya found herself worrying less and less about the burned coffee. "Thank you."

"You're going to be a big help to the program. I can tell," he said to his coffee cup.

It was just as well. Anya was probably grinning like an idiot, and Brock didn't need to see that.

"I'd like to do something to return the favor." He looked up at her. "I think it's time I meet this dog of yours. I can show you some things to help her come out of her shell. Okay if I come by your place tomorrow?"

Anya blinked at him wordlessly. The thought of Brock Parker in her house gave her pause. To put it mildly, it wasn't a good idea. Not at all.

He was too handsome. Too heroic. And to her utter astonishment, she realized she'd even come to think of him as too cute in those crazy get-ups of his.

And she was too…

Too what? she wondered. Too jaded? Too attracted to him?

Too afraid?

She swallowed. Bingo.

Even so, she found herself agreeing. "That sounds good."

"Okay then."

With a shaky hand, she jotted down the number of her cottage. And as Brock slipped it into the pocket of his parka, Anya couldn't help but wonder just what she'd gotten herself into.

Chapter Seven

"Mom, are you home?" Anya wandered down the hall toward the sewing room.

For once, the whirring of the sewing machine hadn't greeted her upon entering the house. She found the silence eerie—alarming, in a way—as though she'd accidentally walked into the wrong home.

"Of course I am," her mother called out. "Where else would I be?"

"Good question," Anya muttered as she leaned against the doorframe of her old bedroom and let her gaze fall on her mother.

As usual, she was bent over the sewing table. Only this time, her stitches were silent. Done by hand. Reading glasses were perched on the tip of her nose, and she still held the fur cuff of the parka she was working on only inches from her face.

"One of these days, I'm going to give up working

with fur. I've already poked myself three times." She peered at Anya over the top of her glasses. "What brings you by?"

Anya shrugged. "Nothing in particular."

It was the truth, yet it wasn't. She'd hoped to tell her mom she'd been back on the mountaintop. And had survived to boot. She wanted to tell her mom all about Sherlock and Aspen. And yes, Brock too. But now that she was here, she was inexplicably bashful.

Are all families like this? Or just mine? Why is it so hard to talk to her?

"You have something to say." Her mother abandoned her sewing and slid the reading glasses off. "I recognize that look on your face. What's got you so excited?"

Anya took a deep breath. "I've begun volunteering with the ski patrol."

Her mother's eyes grew wide. And wary. "What?"

"I'm helping out with the ski patrol. They've acquired two new avalanche search dogs, and I'm working with the patrol to get them trained and ready for duty." Before her mother could respond, she launched into a detailed explanation of the training she'd done with the pups.

She started by telling her mom all about reading the newspaper aloud and hand-feeding. Before long she'd relived the whole snow machine outing and how she had felt when Sherlock had found her in the trench. "You should have seen him, Mom. He was so excited to find me. He's such a great dog. And who knows? Maybe someday he'll find a real avalanche victim…actually save someone's life. And I'll have been a part of that."

"You certainly seem excited about all this. I can't believe you've been back up there." Her mother shook her head. She didn't say a word about why Anya's willingness to go back up the mountain came as a shock. She didn't have to. Speed's unspoken name hung in the air, just as Anya's father's name had for as long as she could remember.

"Me neither," Anya said. "It's been fine, though. Really, it has."

Her mother cleared her throat. Quite forcefully. Undoubtedly, a change of subject was in order. No talking about the past. It was the unwritten rule of the household.

"However did you get involved with this?" Anya's mother angled her head. "I can't even imagine."

"It's kind of a funny story actually." Anya suppressed a grin as she thought of Brock and his bear suit. Perhaps she should leave that detail out of the story. She doubted her mother would find it humorous. "I was looking for someone to help with Dolce, and Clementine led me to Brock."

"Brock?" His name almost sounded like a dirty word coming from her mother's mouth. "Who is this Brock?"

Oh boy. "He's an avalanche expert and he trains

dogs in search and rescue. He just moved here. The ski patrol hired him to head up their search and rescue program. He's been teaching me how to get Dolce to come out of her shell."

She specifically didn't mention her impending eviction from the cottage. Now didn't seem like the best time to throw that problem into the mix.

"Anya." Her mother sighed.

Anya stiffened. Why had she come? She should have known her mother wouldn't understand. Yet here she was, trying to explain how exciting it felt to be a part of something so important. Trying, but apparently not succeeding. "Mom, it's not what you're thinking."

"Oh, really? What am I thinking?"

"There's nothing going on between Brock and me." Why was she constantly saying this? Whatever fleeting moments of attraction she'd experienced were unilateral. The man wouldn't even look her in the eye. Unless he was attracted to her forehead, there wasn't anything to worry about.

"I don't want you to get hurt. That's all. What do you really know about this man?"

I know he believes in me. "He's trained dogs all over the world to save people. Everyone calls him a hero. I think that's enough to believe he can help my dog. Don't you?"

"I don't know, Anya…"

"Well, I do." She knew she'd finally found something that made her happy. Something worthwhile. And for right now, knowing that was enough. "I have to go. I just wanted to come by and tell you about the ski patrol."

"Stay for dinner?"

"I can't, Mom. I have plans." She concentrated unnecessarily hard on zipping up her parka and pulling on her mittens, afraid to meet her mother's gaze lest the plans she'd made with Brock were visible in her eyes. It was ludicrous. She felt like a thirteen-year-old. "Besides, it looks like you've got a lot of work to do."

"Always." Her mother slid the reading glasses back in place, and her lips fell into a flat line.

Always.

She's right, Anya thought as she left her mother to her sewing. *Things around here never change.*

"That's it?" Anya cocked her head.

Brock was acutely aware of her gaze sweeping him up and down as he stepped inside her cottage. Situated behind the main building of the Northern Lights Inn, it was one of a series of tiny bungalows that overlooked the frozen expanse of lake where the ski planes so typical of Alaska landed to unload their cargo.

"Pardon?" he asked, ignoring her scrutiny and taking in the surroundings.

Cozy, he mused. From the fluffy pillows and

polka-dotted throw covering the sofa, to the half-dozen or so balls of yarn arranged in a bowl on the coffee table, Anya's home was filled with color. Bright turquoise, vibrant magenta, lime green and strawberry red. A bit girly for his taste, but it definitely beat the stark white walls, brown leather sofa and pile of cardboard boxes he called home.

"I said, 'is that it?'" Anya crossed her arms and aimed her gaze at the space above his head. "No antlers? I'm disappointed. You're losing your edge."

He grinned, despite the lecture he'd given himself on the drive over that this visit was strictly business, not a social call. "I told you that was a socialization exercise."

"Whatever." She lifted one slender shoulder in a shrug, teasing him.

Yet Brock noticed her heart wasn't in it. She looked a little...sad. He frowned and found himself wondering what had happened to make those eyes of hers lose their trademark sparkle.

Stop it. Anya's problems—whatever they might be—are none of your concern. You're not here to be her friend. To act as if you were would be unfair.

Unfair or not, it didn't seem right to proceed with dog training business. In fact, it seemed insensitive—not to mention downright unkind—to ignore that lost look on her face.

"Everything okay?" He cleared his throat. Could

this get any more awkward? "You don't seem to have your usual enthusiasm for mocking me."

"You noticed?" She lifted a brow, clearly shocked he would ask about her well-being.

Join the club. You're not the only one. "Yes, I did."

"Thank you for asking," she said warily. "Nothing major. I just came from my mother's. Family baggage, I guess you could say."

He nodded, not quite sure how to respond.

"All families have issues, I suppose. You know what I mean, right?" She gazed up at him with those soulful eyes, and before Brock knew what he was doing, he let his guard down.

"All too well, I'm afraid." The words were out before he even realized what he'd said.

He had the very sudden, very real urge to reel them back in. Brock didn't talk about his brother. To anyone. Ever. And he wasn't about to start now, even if something about Anya gave him the vague impression that they might be kindred spirits.

Impossible. On the surface, they didn't appear to have much in common. Even if there was some mutual ground he had yet to discover, Brock doubted it would have anything to do with something as morbid as a family member's kidnapping. At least he hoped not—for Anya's sake.

She breezed past him, and he exhaled a sigh of relief. Whatever her family baggage involved, she didn't seem any more ready to discuss it than he did.

"Would you like some hot chocolate?" She paused at the doorframe. Light spilled from the kitchen, bathing her in a warm, homey glow that made it difficult for Brock to swallow.

"Um, sure. Thanks." Instead of following her he waited in the living room and tried to get his bearings.

This wasn't a date. He was here to help her dog. A dog he'd yet to lay eyes on, he couldn't help but notice. Anya wasn't kidding when she said the pup was shy.

Still, he couldn't help but feel a little like a jerk knowing she was in there pouring him a cup of cocoa. In all the times she'd been to his home, he'd never offered her so much as a glass of tap water.

After another moment, Anya returned with a mug in each hand.

He took one. "Thank you."

"You're welcome." She took a sip of hers. "So Mr. Miyagi, would you like to meet my dog now?"

"Lead the way, er…young protégé."

"Daniel." She shot him a grin over her shoulder as she guided him to what he supposed was her bedroom. "His name is Daniel."

"I guess I'm not up on my eighties movie trivia."

"You're in serious need of a movie marathon." Anya rolled her eyes. At least Brock thought she did. He was doing his best to keep his focus on her forehead. Things were already getting a little too cozy without the added distraction of those eyes.

Anya didn't seem to notice. She sank, cross-legged, to the floor and gave the space beside her a pat.

Brock sat down and gestured to the Bible, magazine and ball of lime-green yarn—speared through with knitting needles—littering the floor beside the bed. "It looks like you've been spending some time down here."

"It's working." She grinned and pointed to the small, black, quivering nose resting on a pair of white paws that poked out from under her bed. "See?"

Brock waited a beat for the rest of the dog to make an appearance. When it was clear all he was going to get was a nose and a pair of paws, he frowned. "So this is progress?"

"Yes. Haven't you noticed? She's quiet." Anya nodded. "And when I feed her, she crawls almost halfway out."

"Why don't we offer her a treat then?" Brock reached in his pocket. "Here, take a couple."

Anya wiggled her nose. "Wow, these are certainly…fragrant. What are they?"

"Dried salmon." Brock placed a few of the treats in her hand. "Now offer them to her with an open palm. But don't get too close. Let's see if she'll come all the way out to get a nibble."

"Okay," she whispered and did as he said.

The dog's nose trembled, and the rest of her head appeared—pointy ears and markings of wolf grey in a masklike pattern around warm, brown eyes. She resembled a miniature sled dog, quintessentially Alaskan.

Anya moved her palm forward a little, and Brock reached out to still her arm. "No. Just stay where you are. Let's see if we can wait her out."

Out of the corner of his eye, Brock saw Anya nod. They waited a few moments in silence. Not wanting to look right at the dog and intimidate her, Brock searched for another place to fix his gaze. He settled on the ball of yarn.

"You knit?" he asked.

"Yes, I belong to a group at church. We make hats for underprivileged folks out in the Bush." Anya's voice was barely above a whisper.

Brock knew she was simply trying not to frighten the dog, but something about that breathy whisper unnerved him just the same. He cleared his throat and stared into his mug of hot chocolate. He didn't dare look at Anya. Or the dog.

"How long have you had her?" He pointed the toe of his hiking boot toward the dog.

"About a year."

"A *year?*" Brock sputtered and nearly choked on a marshmallow. "Are you serious?"

"Sure, why?" She blinked at him innocently with those lovely violet eyes.

Brock looked back down at his mug. "That's an extraordinarily long time. Most people would have given up on this dog by now."

"Given up? *Given up?* That's horrible. I would never give up on her. I rescued her off the streets. She doesn't have anyone but me." Anya's voice grew a little wobbly. From the sound of things, if Brock ventured a glance at her he wouldn't have been surprised to see a tremble in her bottom lip. "I could never just abandon her."

Clearly his remark had struck some kind of nerve. "Your devotion to her is admirable."

"Not really." She sniffed. "It's the right thing to do, that's all."

The right thing to do.

Bits and pieces of his soul-searching with the Bible out at the ski patrol headquarters came back to Brock. With a pang, he remembered convincing himself he was doing God's work. Somehow, sitting here on the floor beside Anya and her dog, it sounded rather arrogant.

"Of course, I may not have a choice in the matter. Time is running out." She sniffed. "She's making progress, though. I think the toy you gave me is helping. There weren't any complaints about her while I was at work today."

"I'm glad." Brock's head spun. He hadn't realized

exactly how bad the situation had gotten. Surely there was something else he could do to help. "What's her name?"

"Dolce." In the split second before Brock focused on her forehead, he saw a glow of pure affection in her eyes. "It means *sweet* in Italian."

They weren't in Italy, and the dog wasn't sweet. Dolce was a name for fluffy white dogs who rode around in women's handbags in places like New York or Paris. Not dodgy strays that hid under beds, ate their food in the dead of night and managed to push their rescuers to the brink of eviction.

But Brock wasn't about to point out the obvious. He'd seen that look in Anya's violet eyes—the one that told him she thought the sun rose and set on Dolce's shoulders. He wasn't going to be the one to burst her bubble.

Dolce had no idea how good she had it. From the look of things, Anya would walk across burning coals for that dog.

For a moment, just a moment, Brock wondered what it would be like to inspire that kind of devotion in a woman.

This woman, in particular.

Before he could process that sudden wish, Dolce scooted out from beneath the bed. She shimmied on her belly, making her way toward Anya's hand.

Brock grinned and Anya gasped in delight as

Dolce scooted alongside her leg—the one farthest from Brock—and began eating from her hand.

Anya beamed at him. "Thank you."

"This is your doing. Not mine." Brock swallowed with great difficulty. "So let me get this straight. When you're not making the best coffee in Aurora, you're helping me with the ski patrol, knitting hats for poor people and rescuing frightened dogs?"

She laughed. "It's only the one."

He handed her a few more treats. "One what?"

"One hat and one dog." She shrugged. "I'm kind of new at this…faith and making a difference."

"It suits you," he said in a voice almost too quiet for her to hear.

Who was he kidding? This was more than just business.

He hadn't asked for it, but Anya had crawled under his skin. His reluctance to admit it didn't change the fact that they were becoming friends.

Close friends.

Dolce finished her treats, and Brock breathed a sigh of relief when she nestled into Anya's side instead of retreating under the bed. He had a feeling he was going to be here a while, which was perfectly fine.

The moment was so perfect that part of him—the best part, probably—wanted it to last a very long time. He reached for Anya's hand and gathered it in his own.

Her skin was warm. And soft. So, so soft.

"Can I ask you something?" she whispered.

"Sure."

There was a long pause, then finally, "Why don't you ever look me in the eye?"

Because those eyes are so beautiful I'm afraid I'll lose myself in them.

Brock cleared his throat. "Does it bother you that I don't?"

"Yes, very much." She turned to look at him.

He looked right back into her eyes, which seemed bigger and more luminous than ever before. "Then I will from now on."

Brock had barely made it home when his cell phone rang. For a single, delusional moment he thought perhaps he'd hear Anya's voice on the other end.

"Hello?" he ground out, wondering what was happening to him—when he'd begun to think it was a good idea to hold hands with someone he worked with or to wish he'd hear her voice on the phone.

"Brock Parker?" A distinctly nonfeminine voice called out to him over the phone line.

He cleared his throat. "This is Brock."

"This is Guy Wallace, of the Utah Search and Rescue Unit, Mountain Division. I'm glad I reached you."

"Yes?"

"We're looking for some help training a pair of avalanche search dogs. Naturally, your name came up."

"I see," Brock said.

He was accustomed to receiving these types of calls. This was his life after all. But for some reason, he wasn't all that interested in talking to Guy Wallace from Utah at the moment.

"We'd love to fly you out here and show you around. We've got a fine pair of pups, ready and waiting to be trained. Frankly, I'm a little out of my element and could use some assistance."

"What kind of dogs?" Brock asked.

"Nova Scotia Duck Tolling Retrievers."

Same as Sherlock and Aspen. Tempting. Very tempting.

This was the type of situation that had Brock's name written all over it. Still, he hesitated. It took a moment for him to think of something to say. "What's your avalanche threat level?"

"Moderate. Our snow has been light this year so far. I don't think we're in any immediate danger, but it's a good time to get some serious training in. And like I said, we've got these pups."

No immediate danger. Relief coursed through Brock. "I'm actually in the middle of a job right now. Up in Alaska."

"When do you expect to be free?" Guy asked.

"I can't really say. We've got a ways to go. Months, most likely."

Months? That was a stretch. Things were progressing in Aurora right on schedule. Sure, Sherlock was proving to be more of a challenge than he'd expected. But Brock could fix that soon enough. What was he saying?

"Well, keep us in mind if things change. And give me a call when you have an exit date. I'm sure we can accommodate your schedule. According to everyone I've spoken with, you're the best."

Brock took down Guy's contact information, writing it carefully in the notepad he kept in the pocket of his parka. "Thank you, sir. I'll be in touch."

Chapter Eight

The buzz of a ski plane landing on the frozen lake behind the Northern Lights Inn snapped Anya out of her daydream. She removed her elbows from the counter, stood up straight and smoothed her apron.

Since Brock's visit to her home the night before, she'd been hopelessly distracted. This morning she'd even given Gus, one of her regular customers, a generous portion of caffeinated Gold Rush bold blend instead of his customary watered-down decaf. The old man's eyes had just about popped out of his head after one sip.

She ventured a glance at Gus now as he climbed down from the cockpit of the single-engine ski plane that had skidded to a stop moments before. He appeared to be back in good form.

Good, she thought. She didn't want to be responsible for debilitating Aurora's one and only Bush pilot. She was in enough trouble as it was.

Anya inhaled a steadying breath and went to work scrubbing the surface of the espresso machine as if she were trying to scrub the brushed nickel finish right off. She wished her growing feelings for Brock could be scoured away with a little elbow grease too. Because even though everything within her railed against the idea, she was developing an affection for him.

Because he'd been the one to notice.

Brock had known her a matter of weeks, and somehow he'd seen the changes she'd been making in her life since she'd come to know God.

Brock had noticed.

And by all appearances, he liked those changes.

For some reason, it was this knowledge that Brock saw in her that weakened her resistance. Ever so slightly.

"Whoa, take it easy there. What did that machine ever do to you?" Clementine grinned and gestured to the Gaggia as she slid onto one of the barstools on the opposite side of the coffee bar.

Anya dragged herself from her thoughts and smiled at her friend. "I'm doing a little deep cleaning this morning. No biggie."

She gave the machine a final swipe with her dishrag and exhaled a relieved breath. She couldn't have been happier to see Clementine—anything to take her mind off Brock. Anya had never been the kind of woman to moon over a man, and she wasn't about to start now. "Can I interest you in a Macaroon Mocha, today's special?"

"Yes, please. You know me so well." Clementine slid her purse from her shoulder and plunked it down on the empty barstool beside her. "So how are things going?"

"Great. A little slow today, though." Anya pumped a few squirts of coconut syrup into the latte cup. Then, because it was Clementine, she added a couple more for good measure.

"I'm not talking about business." Clementine cast a glance over her shoulder at the near-empty lobby. "I mean how are things going with Dolce? Are you still seeing Brock?"

Anya's face flushed with warmth at the question, which was absurd. She wasn't seeing him. And she had no intention of doing so, even if holding his hand had made her feel more womanly than she'd felt in a long time. Feminine. Special.

A familiar phrase leapt out at her from years ago—*no one special.*

She swallowed and pushed Clementine's coffee across the counter. "Yes, Brock's still helping me out."

"Are you learning anything? Or is he still just having you read aloud to his dogs?"

"I'm learning quite a bit, believe it or not. I've been sitting next to my bed every day when I get home, just hanging out, reading, knitting. And it's working. Dolce's even crawling out from under the bed now to sit beside me."

Clementine's mocha paused en route to her mouth. "You're kidding."

"Nope." Anya shook her head. "I'm not."

"I have to say I'm surprised. I've helped Ben rescue lots of sled dogs from the animal shelter, and none of them have ever taken this long to come around."

Her words reminded Anya of Brock's shocked expression when he'd found out how long ago she'd rescued Dolce...and his comment about how most people would have given up on her. The idea was still so inconceivable to Anya that it brought a pang to her heart. "You know, I always thought Dolce was some kind of miniature husky, but Brock says she's not. He said she's an Alaskan Klee Kai."

Clementine's brows drew together. "I've never heard of that breed before."

"Don't feel bad. I'm from Alaska, and I've never heard of it before either. Brock says they're notoriously shy, which is probably part of the problem with Dolce. But he thinks she may have been abused for a while, more than just the one time I witnessed." The notion made Anya sick to her stomach, even though she'd suspected as much before she'd enlisted Brock's help.

Clementine reached across the counter and rested

her hand on Anya's. "Dolce's lucky to have you. You know that, right?"

"I'm the lucky one." Anya firmly believed it. She didn't know what she would do without the dog. And her attachment had grown even stronger since Dolce appeared to be coming around.

"Well, I couldn't be happier things are working out." Clementine took a generous sip of her mocha. "When will I ever get to meet the dog genius?"

"He keeps to himself a lot." Anya tried to remember when she'd seen him out and about. Aside from their training sessions and his occasional visit for coffee, not at all.

She wondered why that was. Brock's dogs apparently weren't the only ones who needed socializing.

"He's going to the Reindeer Run tomorrow, isn't he?" Clementine asked as if it were a foregone conclusion.

"I don't know. He mentioned it the other day, so maybe."

"Maybe?"

Anya couldn't help but laugh at the look of shock on Clementine's face. "Believe it or not, running through the street with a bunch of loose, antlered animals isn't on everyone's bucket list."

"Of course it is. This is Alaska." Clementine shrugged. "You're still going, right?"

"Oh, I'll be there watching from the sidelines. I wouldn't miss it." Anya crossed her arms and narrowed her gaze at her friend. "Tell me, does your husband know you're planning on running in this thing?"

Clementine laughed. "Ben is well aware. He's not crazy about the idea, but he knows better than to try to come between me and a bunch of reindeer. He's running with me. You should join us. We could form a team."

Anya shook her head. Poor Ben. Clementine's adventurous streak had a tendency to bring out his protective nature. Anya wasn't about to put herself in the middle of a marital squabble, no matter how happy the two of them clearly were. "That's okay. I'll sit this one out and take photos of you and Ben getting trampled."

"That might make a good Christmas card picture." Clementine winked and slid her empty coffee cup across the bar. She gathered her handbag and waved as she turned to go. "See you tomorrow."

Anya waved back. "Tomorrow."

Before Clementine had disappeared from view, Anya's thoughts turned once again to Brock. Would he be there tomorrow too? She hoped so. Not because she was anxious to see him again. Of course not. She just had a feeling he'd give those reindeer a run for their money.

"So, what do you think? Are you up for a run this morning?" Brock asked.

Aspen cocked his head but made no move to spring to his feet. The pup remained sprawled on his belly on the braided rug that Brock had finally unearthed from inside one of the cardboard boxes and tossed on the floor. Aspen and Sherlock had immediately become engaged in a turf war over the shabby thing, which Brock had picked up a few years ago at a street market in Italy. Or was it Austria? He wasn't sure. After a while, all the places seemed to run together.

He shoved his feet in his running shoes and frowned. For some odd reason, he'd been unable to get anyone to give him a straight answer as to the distance of the Reindeer Run. The whole town appeared to be getting geared up for the event, so he doubted the route would be more than a 5K. Still, the idea of tromping through three miles of shin-deep snow in a pair of Nikes was unappealing at best. He abandoned the running shoes in favor of a worn pair of hiking boots and zipped into his ski patrol parka.

"Sherlock, come on, boy." Brock gave Sherlock's leash a shake, rattling the metal end with a jingle. The pup came bounding from the hallway and slid to a stop at Brock's feet.

Aspen released a half-hearted attempt at a whine.

"Faker," Brock muttered. "I don't feel guilty in the slightest about leaving you behind. I'm sure I'll hear you snoring before the door shuts behind me."

Aspen sighed and rolled onto his back in the center of the braided rug. Brock shook his head and let out a laugh as he ushered Sherlock outside.

He then heaved Sherlock onto his shoulders.

Brock considered every minute of every day a training opportunity. The Reindeer Run was no exception. No doubt the streets of downtown Aurora would be crowded with people. He wasn't about to waste such an opportunity to further socialize the more timid of the two dogs. Besides, he wasn't exactly looking forward to the event. *Team building…* that's how Cole had referred to it.

Brock wasn't interested in being on anyone's team.

That kind of mentality would only make it harder to walk away once the program on the ski mountain was put into place. And things around Aurora were already growing a bit thorny—the biggest thorn being Anya Petrova.

Since that night at her apartment, Brock had decided to put some distance between them. He didn't go around holding hands with the guys at the ski patrol, and the way he saw it, he had no business holding hands with Anya…no matter how nice the feel of her skin against his had been.

Now he'd gone and blown it by asking her if she'd be interested in helping him train the pups up on the mountain.

What had that been about?

He could have enlisted help from any of the other

guys on the patrol. Granted, they didn't seem to have the same rapport with the dogs as Anya did, particularly with Sherlock. And she seemed so enthusiastic about helping people. She would have been the natural choice, if only looking straight into those captivating eyes of hers didn't make his head spin.

Brock told himself he was making too much of the whole thing as he headed downtown with Sherlock still draped over his shoulders. Anya would be a great helper. And it wasn't as though he'd be able to hold her hand while she was zooming out of sight on a snowmobile or hiding in a snow hole, waiting for the dogs to find her. She'd be tucked safely out of arm's reach, where he couldn't touch her. Or kiss her.

Not that he'd thought about kissing her.

Much.

Brock blew out a frustrated sigh as he rounded the corner onto Third Street. He heard a swell of music, and up ahead he caught a glimpse of what looked like a group of giant carrots—with *legs*—running through the streets.

What?

He squinted at a straggling carrot that appeared to be laboring to catch up with the others. Brock slowed to a stop. As he was trying to process the scene, someone zipped past him. Not a vegetable this time. A person. A person with a sign on his back that read *Grandma Got Run Over by a Reindeer*.

"Clearly, this is no ordinary 5K," he muttered to himself.

"Brock Parker," an amused voice called from behind him. "Leave it to you to stand out, even in a crowd of crazy Alaskans."

Anya.

Of course. He would have known that honeyed voice anywhere.

Brock turned around and found her standing with her arms crossed and a look of pure bemusement in her eyes. "Are you aware that you have a rather large dog slung over your shoulders?"

Sherlock's tail beat against the back of Brock's head. He frowned. She'd charmed his dog. How much longer until she charmed him too? "It's a…"

She held up a graceful hand, cutting him off. "Don't tell me…let me guess…it's a *training exercise.*"

"It *is* a training exercise." He shifted his weight and reached up to steady Sherlock, who was wagging to such an extent, Brock was worried he might attempt a flying leap at Anya. "If we have to ski to an avalanche site on the mountain, it's best to carry the dogs like this. Skis and poles can hurt paws if the dogs run too close alongside. Plus, if they're carried they can preserve their energy for the search site."

Anya nodded slowly, taking in his words. "I guess it's just a bonus that it makes you look like a nut."

She was teasing him as usual. Brock wasn't accustomed to being teased. He was surprised to realize he didn't altogether hate it. In fact, he bordered on liking it.

He lifted Sherlock from his shoulders and set him on the snowy pavement. The dog wiggled over to Anya, and she gave him a good scratch behind his ears.

Another carrot trotted past them, waving this time.

"Hey, Anya," said the carrot.

She straightened. "Hi, Zoey. Be careful out there."

"Will do." Zoey the carrot jogged ahead of them.

Brock thought she looked vaguely familiar. Minus the carrot costume.

He huffed out a breath. It came out in a cloud of vapor and hung suspended in the frigid arctic air. "I think someone forgot to send me the memo."

"The memo?" she asked.

"The one about dressing as a vegetable." He lifted an eyebrow at a pair of teenagers walking by with black-and-white cardboard bull's-eyes fastened to their parkas. "Or a target of some sort?"

A look of confusion crossed Anya's delicate features for a moment until a mischievous smile took its place. "No one told you?"

"Told me what?"

Her smile widened, and she bounced on her toes. Something told Brock the gesture wasn't an effort to keep warm. Anya looked gleeful to the point of bursting. "No one told you about your running buddies? Oh, look. Here they come now."

Brock followed the direction of her gaze and was forced to do a double take. Rounding the corner was a herd of caribou, each animal tethered to a human handler by a lead and bridle. And each was sporting a most impressive—and rather pointy—rack of antlers.

Brock gulped. "My running buddies?"

Chapter Nine

Anya tried not to laugh at the look of horror on Brock's face. She really did. But he looked so uncharacteristically rattled, she just couldn't help it.

She laughed. Hard.

And the harder she laughed, the more Brock glared at her. "This is funny? The fact that I've unwittingly signed up to run around with a bunch of antlered wild animals?"

Anya struggled to regain her composure. Not an easy task. "Don't tell me you're scared of a few innocent reindeer? You, the big hero?"

"That's more than a few. Look over there. I see at least two dozen." He pointed at the end of the road, where the caribou were gathered in a tight cluster waiting for the start of the Reindeer Run. "What is this event? The Running of the Bulls, only Alaska style?"

"Yep." Anya nodded, feeling a tad guilty even as

she grinned. She was getting more enjoyment out of this whole ordeal than she really should have.

Brock paled a bit. "Why didn't anyone tell me about this? All this talk about the Reindeer Run, and no one bothered to explain exactly what it is."

Anya had to bite the inside of her cheek to keep from laughing again. "That's easy. There's a good reason no one mentioned it to you."

"And what might that be?"

Anya shrugged. "You're a hermit."

Sherlock yipped. Anya was fairly certain it was a reaction to the caribou, but the timing was such that it sounded oddly like a yip of agreement.

Brock frowned at the dog and then at Anya. "A hermit? Don't you think that's a little extreme?"

She shrugged again. "I never see you out and about. You haven't made any friends since you've been here. Other than me, I mean."

Her face grew hot all of a sudden. She busied herself with pulling her mittens on tighter so Brock wouldn't notice the flush she was sure was settling in her cheeks.

"Well, there's a good reason for that," he said in a measured voice, as though she should know precisely what he meant.

She met his gaze. "What…?"

Before she could get the question out, Brock threw up his hands at a few more carrots sauntering down the snowy sidewalk. "I have to ask—why the carrot costumes?"

"Oh, that's simple. People really get into this, and reindeer love carrots. You'll see all sorts of costumes once you get closer to the starting line. That's why I thought you'd get a kick out of this, given your penchant for crazy get-ups." She swept him up and down with her gaze. "Look at you. You look almost ordinary. If you hadn't been carrying Sherlock on your shoulders, I might have mistaken you for a normal person."

It wasn't altogether true. Brock Parker was hardly ordinary-looking. Even as flustered as he currently was, his piercing blue eyes were so intense they could melt a glacier.

She gulped.

"It's not a penchant. It's training. Specifically, socialization." The same old refrain, but this time a smile tipped his lips as he said it.

"Hey, there you are." Cole Weston, wearing a red ski patrol parka identical to Brock's, approached them. His eyes lit up when he spotted Anya standing beside Brock. "Anya, good morning. Brock here tells me you're going to keep giving us a hand with training the dogs on site."

"Yes." She nodded and rose on her toes, buoyed by thoughts of making a real contribution. "I'm really looking forward to it."

"According to Brock, we're lucky to have your

help. He says you have a real knack for the work."
Cole glanced at Brock, whose expression was unreadable.

Had he really said that about her?

Interesting.

Training was scheduled to resume on Wednesday. Anya had it marked on her calendar in red ink.

Cole turned his attention to Brock. "Come join us at the start line."

"Sure. I'll be right there," Brock said.

"See you in a few." Cole headed down the block toward the quickly growing crowd of runners.

The event was rapidly taking on the atmosphere of a big street party. The participants had started bouncing a colorfully striped beach ball overhead. Every now and then a snowball would whiz past.

Anya watched it all, trying to see it through Brock's eyes. What must he think of Aurora? A swell of hometown pride rose up inside her. Brock had been to all sorts of exotic places, but she was sure he'd never seen anything like this.

He took a step closer, sending Anya's heart into rebellious overdrive.

"Would you mind keeping an eye on Sherlock for me during the race? I wasn't expecting…this." He grinned, clearly at a loss for words, and removed a leather leash from the pocket of his parka. "I'm fairly certain he's never seen a giant carrot before today."

"Of course I'll watch him." She took the leash

from Brock and snapped it on Sherlock's collar. The dog swiveled his cute, foxlike head and watched her every move. "It's good socialization at least," she added, only half-joking.

"That it is." Brock lingered for a moment.

Was Anya imagining things? Or did his hesitation to walk away seem to have little to do with the herd of reindeer awaiting him?

"Be careful out there," she said, wishing she could be around him without experiencing this unwanted feeling of wistfulness. Not only was it distracting, it also was downright annoying. "See you at the finish line. If you survive, that is."

And before he could respond, she turned to go, if only to prove to herself she was fully capable of walking away from Brock Parker.

As Brock waited with the other ski patrol members for the start of the race, he couldn't help but shake his head in wonder. Aurora was turning out to be full of surprises. Running with actual reindeer? He had to admit he'd never heard of that one before. Now that he'd had a moment to digest the idea, it sounded like fun. Crazy, but fun.

"Runners, are you ready?" a voice boomed from the loudspeakers mounted at each street corner.

A collective roar of affirmation rose from the crowd. In addition to the carrots, a number of other costumed runners had appeared—the abominable snowman from that old Rudolph movie, a few folks with moose antlers affixed to their hats and, inexplicably, a group dressed as the cast of Star Trek.

The loudspeaker crackled to life again. "We're going to start the countdown in a moment. As always, we'll give the humans a ten-second head start."

Brock turned to Cole. "Why a head start?"

"The reindeer are very fast." Cole laughed. "There's a trophy for the first runner to cross the finish line, but beating the reindeer isn't in the realm of possibility, even with the head start."

"Really?" Brock glanced at the animals huddled together near the start line.

They were larger than other species of deer Brock had seen before. And he knew that reindeer were special in that both the males and females had antlers. But he hadn't heard anything before about them being particularly agile. Then again, he'd never considered racing one of them before.

"Ten…nine…eight…" The countdown began, and Brock's fellow racers joined in. Soon everyone around him was shouting along. "Four…three…two…one."

"Here we go," Cole said and started running.

Brock wasn't sure if the plan was for the entire ski patrol to stick together for the duration of the race, or to make a go at winning the trophy. When Cole zipped past him, followed by a determined-looking

Jackson, Brock figured the unit was gunning for the win. He picked up the pace just as the announcer called for the release of the reindeer.

The remainder of the event was a blur. Once the caribou became part of the action, chaos ruled. Cole hadn't been kidding. The animals were ridiculously fast. Fortunately, they were also adept at avoiding the runners. In the beginning, Brock concentrated on running as fast as he could. When he realized outrunning them was indeed hopeless, he switched his strategy to keeping an eye out for antlers over his shoulder. But every time a reindeer came into his peripheral vision, it rocketed past him before he could even formulate a plan to get out of its way.

The race was only five blocks or so, which was plenty considering the abundance of snow. At times Brock felt as though he were trudging through Jell-O rather than running. So it came as a genuine surprise when he realized he was the first human participant in the Reindeer Run to cross the finish line.

"Congratulations!" the announcer said, slapping him on the back. Brock recognized him from the *Yukon Reporter* as the mayor of Aurora. "You're the winner of the fifth annual Reindeer Run."

"Thank you, sir." Brock took the trophy the mayor offered him. It featured a small gold runner on a wooden base, like any other track-and-field trophy. Unlike any other trophy, however, antlers sprouted from its sides.

It was one of the goofiest things Brock had ever seen. Ridiculous looking, really.

Brock loved it.

He was surrounded at once by what felt like half the town of Aurora, offering words of praise and congratulations. As Brock took it all in, a feeling came over him that he couldn't recall experiencing in a very long time, if ever. He was disconcerted to realize the pleasant sensation was one of belonging. Like he was part of something...or some place.

A stab of worry pricked his consciousness.

Was he becoming socialized? Like one of his dogs? Surely not.

Still, he couldn't help but wonder what Anya would have to say about the matter.

And then there she was, as if he'd conjured her simply by thinking of her. And Brock was struck with the thought that there were more dangerous things than feeling like he belonged in Aurora.

"It looks like congratulations are in order," she said, smiling up at him with Sherlock leaning against her legs. Snow flurries danced around her face, and her skin glowed in the winter wind, as pink as a rosebud.

A rosebud, Brock? Really? Get a grip on yourself. You wouldn't compare Cole's skin to a rosebud, would you?

"Thank you." He held his trophy aloft. "Beautiful, isn't it?"

"Very." She nodded. "I hope you don't have designs on keeping that thing on your mantel, though. Cole has always wanted someone from the ski patrol to win so they can have one of those for the patrol cabin."

"You think so?"

"Oh, yes. In fact, here he comes now."

"Brock, my man!" As Anya predicted, Cole looked as happy as if Brock had single-handedly held back an avalanche with his bare hands. "You did it. We won!"

His use of the word *we* settled in Brock's gut with all the buoyancy of a lead weight. Not that he cared a whit about handing over his trophy to the ski patrol. What would he have done with it after he left Aurora anyway? It wasn't the sort of thing he could imagine dragging from place to place in his modest collection of cardboard boxes.

The term *we* was loaded with implications, though. Implications Brock had always been careful to avoid. He'd never been part of a *we* before.

Was he part of one now?

No, of course not.

"Yes, we did it," Brock managed to force out. "Do you think there's a place for the trophy somewhere in the ski patrol cabin?"

"Are you kidding? Of course there is. I have the perfect spot in mind." Cole flashed him a thumbs up.

"I'm sure you do," Anya said with an amused roll of her eyes. "How long have you wanted that trophy?"

"Five long years." Cole shook his head. "I guess it took Brock coming here from halfway around the world to win it for us."

One by one, the other members of the ski patrol crossed the finish line. A few other locals trailed behind them but most notably a couple who were clearly friends with Anya.

She grinned as they jogged to a halt and wrapped them both in tight hugs. "Clementine, Ben! You two made good time out there."

The woman—Clementine—cast a curious glance in Brock's direction before turning her attention back to Anya. "We did. I think Ben was trying to get it over with as quickly as possible. Who's your friend?"

Anya flushed. Or perhaps it was the wind that brought out the pink in her cheeks. "Clementine, Ben, this is Brock Parker."

"Pleased to meet you." Ben nodded and pointed at Brock's trophy. "Nice work."

"Thank you," Brock said.

"Yes, congratulations, Brock." Clementine gave Sherlock a pat and greeted him with a smile that told Brock she'd already heard a thing or two about him.

Brock was still wondering how to feel about this unexpected familiarity when Cole and Jackson returned to flank him on either side.

"A celebration is in order, don't you think?" Jackson asked. "Maybe we should all head over to the Northern Lights Inn. Rumor has it they have killer coffee over there." He winked in Anya's direction.

She laughed. "Nice try. I'm off today. But no worries—the coffee bar's covered. Zoey is on the schedule this afternoon, assuming she survives this mayhem."

Cole shrugged. "I can't speak for everyone else, but I'll take my chances. Jackson's right. We do need to celebrate, and maybe if we all gang up on him we can talk Brock here into staying on."

"Staying on?" Anya's face, so recently pink and colorful as if kissed by the wind, paled.

"You don't think I'm going to give up that easily, do you?" Cole nudged Brock and gestured to the trophy, which suddenly seemed immensely heavy in Brock's hands, as though it carried the weight of the entire town of Aurora's expectations. "Not after you showed those reindeer who's in charge."

Brock was vaguely aware of every pair of eyes in the winner's circle turning toward him, watching, waiting. But only Anya's eyes seemed to really see him, threatening to penetrate the armor around his inner self he'd so carefully crafted over the years.

She blinked, and he could see a world of hurt inside those eyes. "Staying on? I don't understand."

Before he could say a word in response, a flash of light erupted in his face.

"Say cheese," a camera-wielding stranger said.

He blinked a second or two late, and he was blinded by another flash.

"Brock Parker, winner of this year's Reindeer Run," said the reporter. "Tell us, do you think you'll be able to repeat your victory next year?"

Brock shook his head and frowned. Spots, after-effects of the camera's bright flashes, swam in his vision. "No, I won't be here next year."

"I don't understand." The reporter leaned closer. "You don't plan on defending your title?"

"No." Brock had no other choice but to spell things out. "I'm not planning on staying in Alaska more than a month or two. I'm only here temporarily."

Just in case that wasn't clear enough, he added, "I'll be long gone by this time next year."

Anya's hand went limp, and Sherlock's leash slipped from her fingers. She stared down at the strip of leather making a dark streak through the snow and knew she should pick it up. But she couldn't bring herself to form a coherent thought, much less move.

I'll be long gone by this time next year...

What in the world did that mean? Anya couldn't begin to wrap her mind around the answer, as obvious as it was.

She couldn't even bring herself to breathe until

the reporter had left. This little scene—so cheerful only moments before—had grown way too familiar. Heartbreakingly so.

As if sensing her distress, Sherlock pressed into her legs, nearly toppling her. The dog clearly wasn't going anywhere, leash or no leash. Even so, Brock bent down to pick it up.

"You'll be long gone? What does that mean, Brock?" Anya searched out his gaze as he straightened. The fact that he no longer looked her in the eye wasn't lost on her.

"You know," he said quietly.

"No. No, I don't know." Anya's voice rose an octave.

The other members of the group appeared at a loss for what to do or say. As they looked back and forth between Brock and Anya, the air grew thick with tension. Anya knew it could only be her imagination, but the snow flurries even seemed to swirl in slow motion.

Brock glanced up for the slightest moment, his gaze landing square in the center of her forehead. *Just like old times,* she thought without a trace of sentimentality. "I'm here to set up the avalanche search team. Remember?"

"Of course I remember," she huffed. "I'm helping you do just that."

"Anya." Clementine lay a hand on her arm.

Anya looked at it, thinking its presence should be at least somewhat comforting. But it wasn't.

"I'm here to do a job," Brock said. "A very specific one."

He sounded business-like. Different from how Anya had ever heard him before.

A collection of memories flooded her mind. Impressions, really, rather than memories—Brock answering his front door in his bear suit, the way she'd come to associate him with the smell of sawdust and puppies, his remarkable talent for transforming an ordinary piece of wood into something beautiful. And last but certainly not least, the feel of Brock's hand—so big, so strong—as it cradled hers.

She swallowed.

"There's more. Go ahead. Say it," she whispered, her voice coming out hoarse, as if she'd been screaming on the outside in addition to the inside.

Cole cleared his throat. "Anya, Brock signed on for…"

Brock cut him off with a sharp look before turning gentler eyes toward Anya. So gentle that she knew for certain she didn't want to hear whatever he was about to say. "I'm here to set up the program, and then I'm moving on. This was always the plan from the very beginning."

"From the very beginning," Anya repeated, wishing she could turn back time to that first day so when Brock answered his door in that crazy bear suit she could skip all the nonsense and get straight to the point: *Can you help my dog...oh, and by the way, are you here to stay or not?* "But…"

But what?

But sometimes when I look at you I feel dizzy.

But you held my hand.

But I want you to stay.

"But you never told me," Anya whispered.

She knew it was unfair to put him on the spot like that in front of everyone. Cole and Jackson were his coworkers, and he'd only just met Ben and Clementine. What must they be thinking? She was fully aware she was acting like a spoiled child. But she was powerless to stop herself, humiliating as it was.

What was wrong with her? Brock had held her hand. It wasn't as though he'd made her any promises. Or kissed her.

But she'd wanted him to. And she hadn't wanted anything of the sort in a long, long time.

"I thought you knew." Finally, Brock leveled his gaze at her. "I'm sorry."

"You're leaving," she said flatly.

Brock didn't utter a word. He remained as silent and still as a statue. It was as though Michelangelo's David had come to life on the streets of Alaska. With the addition of a good parka, naturally.

"Now let's not put the cart before the horse," Cole said calmly. Too calmly. The sound of his voice made Anya want to jump out of her skin. "Our good buddy will be here for a while. There's still a lot of work to do before the program is put into place. And I'm still holding out hope that Brock will change his mind. He'll always have a job here. All he has to do is say yes. Right?"

Cole raised his eyebrows at Brock and rested a hand on his shoulder.

And in that moment Anya saw what she'd been unable to see before—the tension in Brock's sculpted jaw, the guarded look in his ice-blue eyes and the resistance in his posture.

A shadow had crossed over Brock's face the instant Cole suggested he might stay. Brock might be here now, standing directly in front of her. He might have stood in her little apartment with his wide, heroic shoulders filling the doorframe of her kitchen. He might have sat on her bedroom floor and held her hand. But he had no intention of staying in Aurora.

Anya could see it now, plain as day. How had she not known? Brock might still be in Alaska, but he already had one foot out the door.

Clementine slipped her arm through Anya's. "Why don't you come home with Ben and me? I'm sure you don't want to hang out at the coffee bar on your day off."

"I love the coffee bar, even on my day off. You all go on ahead, though." Anya took a deep inhale of frosty air and gulped it down, wishing it would make her numb so she would no longer care about anything. Least of all Brock Parker. "I don't feel much like celebrating. And I need to head home and check on Dolce."

"Anya," Brock said, her name sounding like a plea on his lips.

He wanted her to come along. At least Anya thought he did. She'd stopped listening to anything he had to say. She just couldn't. Not anymore.

"I'm fine. Really. This was fun, but I'm beat. Bye, all." She waved and backed away before she caved and succumbed to the protests of the others. Their words swirled around her like snowflakes, a verbal blizzard.

And all she really wanted was shelter from the storm.

Chapter Ten

Anya couldn't bring herself to go home. She simply couldn't face the emptiness of her cottage. Not after what had just happened at the Reindeer Run.

If she could have burrowed in the sofa cushions with Dolce curled in her lap, it would have been tolerable. Pleasant even. But the thought of sitting on the floor next to the bed, waiting for her dog to acknowledge her was too pathetic to even contemplate at the moment. She was tired of being patient. She was tired of working so hard to earn someone's affection. She was just plain tired.

The only thing worse would have been putting on a brave face and showing up at the post-Reindeer Run activities. *No, thank you.*

She couldn't face Brock right now. What must he think of her? She'd acted as if he owed her an explanation. She had no claim on him. She never had. She was nobody to Brock.

No one special.

Her eyes welled up with tears. And for ten seconds, Anya allowed herself to cry. Only ten seconds. No more. Because what was ten seconds, really? No time at all. So crying over Brock for ten seconds didn't make her weak, or pathetic or any of the other things she'd vowed not to become. It just made her…sad. Sad to her very core.

She kept track of the time in her head. After a few shoulder-wracking sobs, she squared her shoulders, took a deep breath and soldiered on. Where she was going was a mystery. She walked and walked, trudging through the snow until she could no longer feel her fingers or toes. She walked until her face grew numb from the biting Arctic wind. But the sadness was still there, clinging to her like frost on a windowpane. It was the only thing she couldn't manage to freeze into submission.

At last she gave up and headed for her mother's house. She figured it was the one place she could go where no one had heard about the spectacle she'd made of herself at the Reindeer Run. And that was no small thing.

"Anya?" Her mother frowned as Anya slipped in the front door. "You look frozen solid. Where have you been?"

"The Reindeer Run was this morning." Anya's teeth chattered with every word.

Her mother glanced at the clock on the kitchen

wall—the same one that she'd used to teach Anya how to tell time. "That was hours ago. Are you trying to catch frostbite?"

"Nnnnnno," she answered, her teeth still chattering away.

She'd had a mild case of frostbite once when she was a kid, the result of an overly ambitious afterschool snowball fight. Her pediatrician had called it frostnip. She could remember the doctor holding her white, tingling hands, rubbing them back and forth, back and forth, for what seemed like forever. She hadn't been able to feel a thing.

So in a way, the idea that she might have frostbite wasn't without merit. If only the areas farthest from the heart weren't the ones most prone to frostbite and not the other way around. What a cruel twist of fate.

"Sit down. I made some chicken soup last night. I'll heat some up for you." Anya's mother pushed gently on Anya's shoulders.

She crumpled in a heap on the sofa. Her mom tugged on the sleeves of her parka, removed it and wrapped Anya in a fleece blanket. It had kittens on it. Kittens sitting in baskets with balls of yarn.

Cute.

Cute, but profoundly odd. Anya had never thought of her mom as the kitten-loving type. But as she sat there, wrapped like a kitten-clad mummy while her mother bustled about in the kitchen, she wondered if perhaps there was a side of her mother she'd never seen before. A softer side. She liked to think there was.

"Here we go." Her mother returned to the living room carrying a TV tray piled with twin steaming bowls of soup, Goldfish crackers and hot tea.

Anya picked up her bowl and took a tentative sip as her mother turned on the television. "Mom, this is delicious. Thank you."

"You're welcome." Her mom paused for a second, remote control in hand, and studied Anya.

Maybe she should say something. Surely her mother was wondering how she'd ended up wandering the frozen sidewalks of Aurora for the better part of the day.

"Brock is going away. He's leaving town," she said, staring into her soup bowl as if the wide egg noodles contained the secret to the meaning of life. *If only.*

Anya braced herself for the inevitable I-told-you-so that was surely coming her way.

"I see," said her mother. She kept her eyes glued to the television, and for that, Anya would forever be grateful.

One glance of sympathy, one kind word, and she might have fallen apart again. And she didn't want to fall apart. Not now. Not ever.

And remarkably, that was it. They didn't exchange another word about Brock the rest of the evening. No I-told-you-sos, no speeches about how men can't be trusted or how history was doomed to repeat it-self. They simply sat side by side, eating soup and watching bad reality television.

It was just what Anya needed.

"Sherlock, get up."

The dog heaved a dramatic sigh and plopped his chin on his paws. His gold eyes darted to Brock for the briefest moment. Other than that fleeting ac-knowledgment, Sherlock gave Brock no indication that he'd heard anything, much less a command.

Brock frowned.

This was not good. Not good at all.

He might have expected such snippy behavior from Aspen, the world's biggest faker, but not Sher-lock. Sherlock might have been the more cautious of the pair, but he'd always been utterly devoted to Brock. Brock had initially considered this a poten-tial problem.

Loyalty was certainly good, particularly for a search dog. But ideally, Sherlock would pledge his loyalty and devotion to whomever was going to be his permanent handler. And that was not Brock. Which was why Anya's work with the dogs had become so important. They were getting exposure to new people, new happenings. Sherlock, in par-ticular, had thrived under her attention.

But that didn't mean he should start ignoring Brock's commands.

"Sherlock, come."

Brock clapped his hands, whistled, cajoled and generally made a fool of himself. All for naught. The dog didn't budge.

Brock sighed, crossed the room and sank to the floor, cross-legged, beside Sherlock. "Hey, bud. Are you feeling okay?"

He rested a hand on the dog's head. It was warm but not too warm. Similarly his gums were pink, eyes clear and nose wet and cool to the touch. In short, everything about Sherlock appeared fine. Physically, that is.

Somewhere at the back of Brock's mind, he had a nagging suspicion about the exact nature of the dog's problem.

"You miss her, don't you?" Brock laid a hand on Sherlock's rib cage, and in the gentle rise and fall of the dog's breath he knew he'd hit the nail on the head.

Anya hadn't come around since before the Reindeer Run three days ago.

Not that Brock blamed her, and not that she'd been formally scheduled to help with the dogs before their next mountain-top training session on Wednesday, but her absence had been difficult to ignore.

She'd been stopping by occasionally on quick, spur-of-the-moment visits to work with the dogs. And Brock had preferred that. The unexpected nature of her training sessions kept the dogs on their toes, preventing them from becoming accustomed to a routine. Because if there was anything routine about search and rescue work, it was its lack of routine. As for Brock, he'd been surprised at how often he found himself glancing at the barn door, wondering when she'd saunter inside, armed and ready with a teasing comment about whatever he was wearing at the moment.

Of course, all of that had been before.

The Reindeer Run had somehow become one of those events that divided time into two distinct categories—before and after. Such a sentiment would ordinarily seem melodramatic to Brock, but he couldn't help the way he felt. And even though he was loath to admit it, he'd come to realize he greatly preferred Before.

"You'll see her tomorrow on the mountain." At least Brock assumed Sherlock would see her then. He hadn't confirmed things with her since Before, but Anya didn't seem like the sort to bail on something so important. Granted, he'd only known her a matter of weeks, but she definitely gave him the impression that she stuck by her commitments.

Still, it would have been nice to talk to her, to see her, before she started hiding in a hole in the snow and he was but one of several people pretending to search for her.

He glanced down at Sherlock once more. The dog slid his dejected gaze toward him and Brock spoke without thinking, the words slipping from his mouth before he could stop them. "I miss her too."

His head throbbed. Saying such a thing out loud was far different from keeping it inside, even if a dog was the only witness to his confession. Because simply saying it was admitting it. So long as his feelings were tucked deep inside, Brock could almost deny they existed. Almost.

The denial was becoming harder and harder to pull off.

He rose to his feet. The way he saw it, he had two choices—either leave Aurora altogether or patch things up with Anya.

Leaving wasn't without its appeal. Maybe he wasn't ready to admit how much he wanted to stay— he'd had enough confessions for one day—but the idea of leaving town seemed extreme. After all, what had really transpired? He'd made a friend. He'd un-wittingly hurt her feelings. Such things weren't the end of the world. They happened every day.

Except deep down, Brock couldn't help but wonder if his behavior had been one hundred percent unintentional. In all the hours they'd spent together, he'd never once mentioned to Anya that he was only in town until the avalanche rescue program was up and running. But he'd seen fit to mention his plans to Cole on numerous occasions. Could he have subconsciously been avoiding such a conversation with Anya?

That was an idea he really didn't care to ponder.

Whatever was going on beneath the surface didn't matter. The bottom line was that he and Anya would be working together. Sherlock's despondency had brought the potential crisis regarding their working relationship into clearer focus. Brock needed to fix things. It was his professional responsibility, plain and simple.

And above all else, Brock was professional. His work defined him.

He walked Sherlock back to the barn and gave both him and Aspen rawhide bones so large, they were nearly comical in proportion. "You two behave while I'm gone."

Sherlock's depression appeared to ebb somewhat as he systematically went to work licking his rawhide chew from top to bottom.

Good.

Things were already looking up. Hopefully, once Sherlock got back on the mountain, he'd be back to his old self. If only smoothing things over with Anya could be so easy to achieve. Brock smiled as he shrugged into his parka, grabbed his keys and headed for his truck. Brock knew dogs. He'd lived and worked with them for the better part of his life. But now he was out of his element. He didn't have a clue about women. Or friendships, for that matter.

As clueless as he was, he knew a rawhide bone

wouldn't do the trick. But unbelievable as it seemed, Brock had a pretty good idea what might.

The third night after the Reindeer Run, Anya sat in what she'd come to think of as her usual spot— on the floor at the foot of her bed. She was midway through a new knitting project, her first to use multiple colors of yarn. She'd started it with Brock in mind. She was using every color of yarn in the rainbow, and the hat was comically oversized, like an old-fashioned stocking cap. It wasn't a Viking hat or a bear suit, but she had a hunch he'd like it as a socialization tool. Of course, when she'd begun the project, she hadn't realized he was only in town temporarily. She wasn't even sure she could finish it before he left. But to abandon it now would only make his impending departure feel more imminent. And that was the last thing she wanted.

Anya knitted away with Dolce nestled in a ball in the middle of her lap. It was all very cozy, and Anya was beginning to wonder when Dolce might see fit to venture into the living room. The tiny dog had become pretty comfortable within the confines of the bedroom. She'd even been relatively quiet. Since she'd introduced Dolce to the rubber food toy, she hadn't received a single noise complaint from the hotel manager.

But Dolce had yet to cross the threshold into the

hallway. As proud as Anya was of her little pup, she sometimes longed for the comfort of her sofa.

There was a knock at the door, and Dolce's ears flattened in alarm.

All in due time, Anya mused as she gathered her knitting together and lifted Dolce off her lap. The dog stretched and opened her petite mouth in a wide yawn before sliding under the bed.

A trickle of worry still passed through Anya every time Dolce returned to her hiding spot, although she felt increasingly hopeful about the dog's future. She'd come so far since Anya had started working with Brock and his dogs.

At the thought of Brock, Anya's chest tightened. She pressed her palm against the place where her heart beat, as if that small amount of pressure could force her feelings back under control.

It didn't work, of course, and her heart all but did a double flip when she swung the door open and found Brock standing on her front porch.

"Hey," he said and cleared his throat. He looked every bit as uncomfortable as Anya felt.

The evening snowfall had grown more intense since the last time Anya had stepped outside, and it swirled furiously around Brock in every direction. He blinked against an onslaught of snow flurries collecting in his eyelashes. His shoulders were already heavily dusted with snow, making him look even bigger and broader than usual. Anya had the fleeting, fantastical thought that Brock had been caught up in a whirlwind, that the winter wind had picked him right up and deposited him on her doorstep.

She was surprised to find him there. Judging by the bewildered look on his face, Brock was rather startled himself.

"Hey yourself." Anya smiled into the bitter cold, and a shiver coursed through her. She crossed her arms and glanced down, embarrassed to realize she was wearing one of her oldest, rattiest sweatshirts, jeans and fuzzy slippers.

As if on cue, Brock's gaze dropped to her feet. "Nice shoes. What are those? Bunnies?"

"Of course not. They're polar bears." She wiggled a foot toward him. Snow piled on top of her slipper, all but obscuring the polar bear's shiny plastic nose. "No self-respecting Alaskan would be caught wearing bunny slippers. Not so long as there are moose slippers, reindeer slippers and bear slippers—both polar and grizzly—to choose from."

"Of course." Brock shook his head. "Point taken."

"You can borrow them sometime if you like. You know you want to. They make great *socialization tools*." She made air quotes around that last part.

He pinned her with a sardonic look. Anya had never been so happy to see a visible display of sarcasm. After the way she'd acted at the Reindeer Run, she didn't know whether or not she and Brock would be able to find their playful dynamic again. Could they still be friends? Would he even want to after she'd embarrassed both of them?

Apparently, he just might.

"Would you like to come in out of the cold?" she asked.

"Thanks," he said and stepped inside. Instantly, her tiny cottage felt two or three sizes tinier. Brock filled the place.

And before Anya could shut the door, a rush of snow came in behind him.

"Wow, it's really coming down out there." She darted to the kitchen and returned with a towel to mop up the mess.

When she bent down, Brock did so at the same time. "Here, let me."

"That's okay. I've got it…" Their foreheads collided. Anya wasn't at all surprised to discover Brock's head was every bit as hard as it looked. "Ouch."

Marble statue? Try concrete.

"Sorry." Brock winced. "Really, let me."

He reached for the towel, and an unmistakable zing surged through Anya at the touch of his fingertips. She straightened, not liking where this was heading at all. Good grief, the man had barely walked through the door and already sparks were flying. Sparks that were by no means welcome, especially now that she knew Brock's future plans didn't include staying in Aurora.

He finished mopping up the slush and rose. He said nothing, of course, but simply stood there. Quiet as always.

Anya angled her head, wishing she didn't have to ask. "Brock, what are you doing here? I don't think you really stopped by in the middle of a snowstorm to borrow my slippers."

A sheepish smile came to his lips. "I brought a peace offering."

"A peace offering?" Anya gulped. "Really?"

"Yes, an apology of sorts." He unzipped his parka and reached inside.

She couldn't imagine what he had in there, but whatever it was made her nervous. "Brock, that's not necessary. I'm the one who should apologize."

"Shhh."

He was shushing her now? Really? Anya crossed her arms. "I'm not a dog, you know."

"I'm quite aware of that." Brock rolled his ice-blue eyes. "But I think you're going to be particularly pleased with this peace offering."

"You sound awfully sure of yourself."

"Oh, I am." With a flourish, he pulled a slender box out of his jacket.

Anya was speechless—a rare occurrence for her. Brock was the one who was usually so economical with his words. Try as she might, for a few silent beats she could do nothing but stare.

She swallowed and finally managed to speak. "I can't believe you did this."

Brock held the DVD up next to his face. "You mentioned I was in serious need of a movie marathon. I thought *The Karate Kid* was the logical place to start. I'm ready to discover the profound mystery of wax on, wax off. Care to join me?"

She was forced to clear her throat as it clogged with emotion. "How I can refuse?"

"Good." He grinned and slid his arms out of his parka.

So this was really happening? After the humiliation of the Reindeer Run and three days of total silence between them, they were just going to cozy up and watch *The Karate Kid*?

It was crazy. They were adults. They should talk things through, have an actual one-on-one conversation about why Brock had failed to mention his future plans. Anya should just bite the bullet and explain why she'd reacted as she did. She should tell him about her father and about Speed. Would it be pleasant? No, of course not. The tough conversations never were.

She watched Brock stroll over to her television. It took him less than four strides to cover the entirety of her living room. And as he slid her favorite movie into the DVD player and Ralph Macchio's silhouette popped up on the screen in all its cranelike glory, Anya decided talking was vastly overrated.

"I'll make us some popcorn." She paused when she reached the entryway to the kitchen. "Butter or no butter?"

He lifted a single eyebrow. "That's seriously a question? What's popcorn without butter?"

"My thoughts exactly." As she popped a bag of popcorn in the microwave, she noticed that her hands were shaking.

What was that all about? They were two friends watching a movie together.

Let's not make more of this than it actually is.

"Need a hand?" Brock poked his head in the kitchen.

She wished he wouldn't sneak up on her like that. His face was far too handsome to come into view without a proper warning. "I think I've got it under control, but thanks."

He lingered anyway, his gaze traveling over her head to the kitchen window where snow beat against the glass, so white and thick that Anya could no longer make out the shape of the Northern Lights Inn lobby, even though it was only a stone's throw away. The corners of Brock's mouth tugged into a slight frown.

Then—because no matter what remained left unsaid, there was one thing she wanted to make very clear—she took a deep breath. "Brock, just so you know, I'm going to be there tomorrow for the training session on the mountain."

"Okay," he said, tearing his gaze from the window, his voice uncharacteristically soft.

"I'll be there, and I was always planning on being there. I wouldn't have bailed on something so important." She swallowed and watched his eyes shine bright blue, bluer than she'd ever seen them before.

"I know," he said simply, as if he'd never had a moment of doubt.

She found this reassuring, this knowledge that he had faith in her, no matter the circumstances. Anya was a stranger to that kind of faith in people. She'd only recently begun to find that sort of faith in God.

Never will I leave you; never will I forsake you.

It was a promise she clung to as if her life depended on it. An impossibly big promise made by an impossibly big God. She couldn't imagine believing a promise like that from a mere mortal…a person…a man.

Certainly not the man standing beside her.

Because hero or not, he'd made it abundantly clear that he didn't make those kinds of promises.

Chapter Eleven

Somewhere between the time the Karate Kid sanded his first floor and painted Mr. Miyagi's house, Brock began to relax. Even with the snow coming down like it was, he eventually forgot to keep a constant eye on the window and the weather outside. The warmth of Anya's cottage, coupled with the sight of Anya's feet propped up on the coffee table in her fuzzy polar bear slippers, loosened something inside him.

And then there was the company.

Even with the giant bowl of popcorn tucked between them on the sofa, Brock was hyperaware of Anya's presence. Every time she laughed at something onscreen, he felt a pang right in the middle of his chest. When it looked as though the Daniel might throw in the towel, she stared wide-eyed at the television with her bottom lip tucked between her teeth. Brock looked away, determined not to take notice of that lip, no matter how pink and shapely it might be. And then, even though she'd admitted to having seen the movie at least a dozen times already, Anya started sniffling toward the end. Brock would have to be blind not to notice how her violet eyes grew even more luminous than usual when filled with unshed tears.

How did she do it? he wondered. How did she let herself go and experience things so wholeheartedly? He'd spent so much of his life guarding his emotions, controlling his surroundings in an effort to prevent himself from being blindsided with crippling hurt as he was when Drew vanished, that he'd ceased to feel altogether.

And here Anya sat, getting all misty-eyed over a movie. Part of him admired her for it. A large part. And somehow Brock knew the dangers of the storm outside were nothing compared to the swirling blizzard of attraction in Anya's cozy cottage.

He wondered if she felt it too and suspected she might when his kneecap first brushed against hers and she jumped.

"Everything okay over there?" he asked, noting the pink flush that settled in the vicinity of her exquisite cheekbones.

"Sure." She slid her gaze toward him, and his stomach tightened as it always did at the sight of those eyes. "Shall I make more popcorn?"

"No, thanks. I'm stuffed."

She picked up the bowl and moved it to the coffee table, and the space between them grew instantly smaller. Brock rested his arm against the back of the sofa. He wasn't sure how it happened, but within moments Anya's head found its way onto his shoulder.

And it was nice—this closeness. Far nicer than Brock had imagined. And despite what he wanted to admit, he'd imagined a scenario like this one. On more than one occasion even.

Anya's hair carried the subtle fragrance of coffee and caramel, and Brock allowed himself a deep, intoxicating inhale. He had the sudden urge to memorize everything about her—the precise shade of her violet eyes, the incredible softness of her dark hair and the way he felt strong enough to take on the world when she was tucked beside him like this—so he could carry those memories with him when he left.

"Brock," she said in a half-whisper, her body rising and falling slightly against him as she murmured his name.

"Yes?" His breath sent a tiny ripple through her hair.

"I want to explain about Saturday, at the Reindeer Run." She grew still beside him.

The difference was subtle, but Brock noticed it nonetheless.

His first instinct was to tell her she owed him no

explanation. After all, hadn't he come to the eventual conclusion that he'd staunchly avoided talking about his future plans when he'd been around her? He'd suspected as much when he reflected on things in the seclusion of his own home, but here, now, it was an undeniable fact.

Even so, if Anya wanted to talk about things he owed it to her to listen.

"Okay," he said and waited.

She spoke softly and kept her head on his shoulder, so he couldn't see her face. "I overreacted. I know I did, and I'm sorry. Deep down, I guess I have this fear that everyone's just going to go away and I'll be left all alone."

Brock couldn't imagine Anya ever ending up alone. Who would be fool enough to leave her?

You would, you idiot.

"Why do you feel that way?" he asked, hating himself at that moment in a way he'd never hated himself before.

"Because it's happened before. My father left when I was a baby. I've never met him. Twenty-six years after the fact, my mother is still angry and refuses to even talk about him. I don't know anything about the man but his name." She sighed. "Sometimes I wonder how the actions of a single person can have such widespread consequences."

So these were the family issues she'd hinted at before. Brock's hands clenched. He may have nearly made a mess of things with Anya, fraying the fragile threads of their newfound friendship, but he couldn't imagine doing something as cold-hearted as walking away from a woman and a baby.

"I'm sorry," he murmured into her hair.

"Oh, there's more." Anya let out a modest laugh, but Brock could feel the pain behind it.

He sat very still and waited for her to continue. For several long moments, the only thing he could hear was *The Karate Kid* soundtrack mingled with the gentle patter of snowflakes against the windows.

At last, she spoke. "I had a boyfriend a few years ago. My first and only. He was a world-class skier. Skiing was everything to him, and when it provided a way for him to leave Aurora he took it and never looked back. But first he dumped me on national television."

Brock blinked, not entirely believing what he was hearing. "On television?"

Wasn't that a bit of cruel overkill? What was wrong with this guy?

"Yep." She nodded. Brock was barely aware of a lock of her hair tickling his nose.

All of his awareness was centered on one thing, and one thing only. As her words sunk in, he was hit with a realization that changed things. All appearances to the contrary, he and Anya were the same. They were two people whose lives had been shaped not by those who lived among them, but by those who were missing.

Whether they'd walked away of their own accord or been taken in the dead of night didn't matter. The result was the same—a hole in the heart waiting to be filled.

Sitting beside Anya, the hole in Brock's heart felt smaller. And he had the sudden, very real urge to heal the one in hers. A storm of emotions churned inside him, fiercer and more frightening than any snowstorm he'd encountered. He felt a dam break, the dam he'd spent the better part of a lifetime constructing—the one holding back all the pain and confusion about his brother's disappearance. And for the first time, he had an urgent need to share himself with someone.

With Anya.

He was ready to tell her everything—what had happened to his brother that dark, snowy night and how afterward everything about him changed. He would explain why he moved around like he did. He would make her understand it wasn't a choice, but that it was a compulsive need that burned inside him—this obsession with the snow and with finding people. An obsession with no known cure.

Although he was beginning to wonder if a remedy might be among the things he searched for.

Brock cleared his throat. "Anya, I…"

Before he could get started, she gasped and bolted

upright. Her dainty hands clutched at the front of his flannel shirt, and her eyes flew open wide.

Brock followed the direction of her gaze, and his eyes landed on a sight that made him forget all that he was about to say. He could do little but shake his head in wonder at an occurrence so rare and unexpected that it took immediate precedence over anything and everything else.

"Well, would you look at that?" he whispered.

Anya's eyes grew shiny behind a veil of tears. "Is this really happening? I can't believe it."

Brock sent up a silent prayer of thanks. "Believe it."

He reached for Anya's hand and gave it a gentle squeeze as the very elusive Dolce tiptoed her way into the living room.

"Has she ventured this far before on her own?"

Brock's question somehow made its way through the fog of Anya's thoughts. The sight of Dolce gingerly walking around the living room, coupled with the unexpected tenderness of Brock holding her hand—the way she'd felt with him the whole evening, actually—was a little much to take in all at once.

"Anya?" he whispered, prompting her to say something in response to his question.

"No. Never." She licked her lips. "What should I do? Should I praise her?"

"Probably not. We don't want to spook her." Brock paused, considering the options. "I don't have any treats on me. Do you?"

"Unfortunately, no. In the kitchen but not on hand." Anya glanced at the empty popcorn bowl on the coffee table.

Only a smattering of unpopped kernels remained. There was nothing edible within reach.

"Okay, I think we should just stay very still and very quiet. We don't want to overwhelm her." Brock tore his gaze from Dolce and focused instead on Anya. "Try to act casual."

Act casual? Right.

It was an awfully tall order. There wasn't a single casual thing about this evening's events…except maybe her fuzzy polar bear slippers.

Anya was beginning to wonder if all of it was a dream. Had Brock Parker really shown up in the middle of a snowstorm, suggesting they hunker down and watch a movie together? And had things started to feel so cozy that she'd ended up snuggling against him? And had she actually told him all the humiliating details of her past?

Her throat grew dry.

She couldn't—wouldn't—dwell on such things now. She'd grown weary of thinking things through. For once she wanted to forget the past, forget the future and simply live in the moment. Because as moments went, this one was pretty good.

Dolce made a tentative circle around the coffee table, her button nose quivering as she neared the empty popcorn bowl.

"Try not to overwhelm her. You may not even want to look her directly in the eyes," Brock murmured. His voice was calm and even. Anya wondered how he could appear so unruffled.

She did her best not to stare. It was terribly difficult. After all, she'd been waiting a year for something like this to happen. When she'd rescued Dolce from that awful man, Anya had imagined the dog romping around her cottage, chasing balls and chomping on squeaky toys. She'd had no idea just how traumatized the poor thing had been.

Would she have still intervened and saved the dog if she'd known what a long road would lie ahead and that she might even lose her cottage? Of course she would have.

She blinked back the sting of tears—grateful tears. The extent to which Brock's arrival in Aurora had changed things for Anya had never been more apparent than at that moment. Watching her timid little dog, now quiet and confident for the first time, willingly venture beyond the confines of the bedroom was more than she'd dared to hope for in so long.

"You did this," she whispered to Brock, her voice thick with emotion. "I can't thank you enough."

Brock gave a slight shake of his head, but Anya

was glad he didn't say anything to try to deflect her gratitude. She wanted him to know just how much this meant to her, although she couldn't quite put it into words. It meant…everything, really.

Dolce's head swiveled in Anya's direction at the sound of her voice. Anya smiled at her dog. And then Dolce's curly sled-dog tail gave a tiny little wag before she scurried back to the safety of the bedroom.

"Oh!" Anya dropped Brock's hand and clutched at his shirt again, the flannel soft beneath her fingers. "Did you see that? She wagged her tail."

"She sure did," Brock said, his voice still barely a whisper, even though Dolce had returned to her hiding spot.

Anya's gaze lingered on where Dolce had been. She was afraid to look away in case the dog poked her head around the corner again. She held her breath for a few seconds and finally allowed herself to exhale when she heard the rustle of the bedspread, likely from Dolce scurrying underneath the bed.

For a moment, she was paralyzed. She could hardly believe she'd just witnessed the breakthrough she'd wanted for Dolce to have for so many months.

Brock's hand found her shoulder. The weight of it, the warmth of it, told her what she'd experienced had been real.

At last she turned around. His face was closer

than she'd expected. Mere inches away. The sight of him so near flooded her senses.

She swallowed with great difficulty. "So that really just happened?"

He nodded slowly but said nothing. Anya could see tiny flecks of gunmetal gray in his blue eyes that she'd never noticed before—and a few lines near the corners of those eyes that seemed to speak of a world-weariness that made her want to do something utterly ridiculous, like cook him chicken noodle soup or knit him a sweater. She should have been relieved to find an imperfection, tiny as it was, on that gorgeous face. Perhaps it leveled the playing field a bit.

She wasn't relieved. Far from it. If she'd thought she was in trouble before, she was drowning in it now. There weren't words to describe the thinness of the ice upon which she walked.

She was reminded of a moose she once saw creeping its way across the surface of the pond behind the Northern Lights Inn. It had been early spring, weeks after the winter's hard freeze had begun to crack and thaw. By nightfall, an audience had gathered around the moose, cheering it on, willing the creature to make it safely to the other side. Anya had prepared hot apple cider for the spectators, serving it in paper cups with cinnamon stick straws. Nearly everyone in town had cheered and toasted with those paper cups when at last the moose stepped off the ice onto safe, solid ground.

Silly moose, she'd thought, long before the moose had reached the midway point of the pond. *Why doesn't it just turn around and go back where it knows it's safe?*

She inhaled a steadying breath.

Sometimes turning around isn't so easy. Sometimes the lure of what's on the other side is just too hard to ignore.

Brock reached up and, with a gentle swipe of his thumb, he wiped a tear from her cheek. His touch sparked something inside her—something she'd ordinarily never allow herself to feel, much less act upon.

Later, she'd blame what happened next on the excitement of Dolce's breakthrough. At present, she didn't care to examine the reasoning behind the pounding of her heart or the way her gaze was drawn to Brock's lips as though they held a world of secrets she wanted to explore. Behind her, snow danced against the windowpane and music swelled from the television. Anya was hardly aware of either of those things.

She was, however, very much aware of how badly she wanted to kiss Brock Parker. It was a longing she felt down to the marrow of her bones. He was right there, scarcely a whisper away. How easy it would be to just lean in and touch her lips to his.

So she did.

At the first brush of her lips against his, one of Brock's hands slipped to the back of her neck. Then the other. He cradled her head in his big, strong hands as tenderly as if she were made of glass.

If he was surprised by her actions, he didn't show it—a fact that only made Anya's heart beat with even greater intensity. And as Brock drew her closer and deepened the kiss, Anya felt herself falling...

Falling...

Falling...

Like the first fragile snowflake of winter, promising a world of glittering beauty after a long, lonely summer.

Brock wasn't quite sure what was happening to him.

In that brief, sweet moment when Anya had rested a steadying palm on his chest and leaned in to kiss him, he should have had the strength to stop her. Less than an hour ago, she'd told him why she reacted as she did after Cole had mentioned Brock wasn't in Alaska to stay. The last thing Brock wanted was to become another in a list of men who'd disappointed her. Who'd left.

So now—especially now—Brock had no business letting her kiss him. He had no business burying his hands in her hair and certainly no business kissing her back as though his life depended on it.

The trouble was, he didn't want to stop her—not before she'd kissed him and certainly not now.

With the touch of her lips, the memory of every exotic place Brock had ever been—every mountaintop, every snow-crusted summit—flew right out of his head. All the angst, the searching and the restlessness that had been a part of him for so long were replaced with the kind of tranquility he'd never before thought possible. There was only the here and now—*this* place, *this* Alaskan range, *this* woman. And the startling reality that if he stayed, it would be more than enough. More than he'd ever dared to imagine.

And as quickly as all those feelings rushed in, grabbing him by the shoulders and giving him a hard shake, they were gone.

Anya pulled away from him, scrambling to the opposite end of the sofa. Her fingertips flew to her lips. "Oh, no. I'm so sorry."

The sudden absence of Anya from his arms sent Brock reeling. He blinked, confused at what had just happened and even more confused by the sudden look of shock and regret on Anya's lovely face. Her fingers were still pressed to her lips, as if she were trying to keep those lips in check, to prevent them from going rogue and kissing him again.

In his state of bewilderment, Brock managed to breathe out, "What?"

"I'm sorry." She stood, smoothing an imaginary

wrinkle on her sweatshirt and taking a giant step backward. Her calf bumped into the coffee table, sending a turquoise ball of yarn tumbling to the floor.

The trajectory of its roll sent it spinning right past her polar bear-clad feet. Brock's gaze snagged on Anya's slender ankles, disappearing in the puffs of white fuzz.

Does she have any idea how adorable she looks in those crazy slippers?

Doubtful. And something told Brock now wasn't the time to tell her as much.

He lifted his gaze once again to her face. Judging from her tormented expression, Anya's thoughts weren't anywhere remotely near her choice of footwear.

Brock held up his hands, as if he were approaching a frightened deer in the forest, and took a cautious step toward her. "It's…"

"Please don't say it's *fine*." Anya shook her head and crossed her arms across her body.

It's fine was exactly what he'd planned on saying. Even though *fine* was a nearly unspeakable understatement.

"But…" he started.

"But it's *not* fine. I kissed you." She drew her bottom lip between her teeth. Brock tried, and failed, to look elsewhere—anywhere but at her mouth.

Yes, you did. You kissed me. And it was incredible.

He angled his head and searched her eyes for any hint that the kiss had affected her the way it had him. But all he saw there was regret. "Anya…"

"It was a mistake." She swallowed. Brock traced the movement of it up and down the graceful column of her neck. "A mistake that won't happen again."

A mistake.

Brock's chest seized. He wasn't sure why.

She was right, of course. The kiss was a bad idea. The worst. Anya couldn't trust him any more than she'd trusted her father or Speed. Brock's job—and his very nature—meant he was destined to repeat their same failures. He would leave, just like all the others. So she was right. The kiss had been a mistake of the highest order.

Then why did he feel so hollow now that it had ended?

He leveled his gaze at her for a long, electrically charged moment and waited for her to change her mind. Brock was certain she would. Could she really stand there and pretend that kiss hadn't meant something? Hadn't she felt it—that all too brief moment of perfection when their lips met?

He knew she had. He could see it in the faint tremor of her hands. That subtle movement was a visible reminder of the hum of life that had traveled through both of them only a moment ago.

He took another step closer and angled his head. "Anya, please."

He was begging now?

Apparently so.

And he wasn't sure what he was begging for. He only knew that he didn't want to see her so upset, so filled with regret.

She lifted her chin and stared back at him, her violet eyes darkening to a deep, troubled purple. "I think it would be best if you went home now, Brock."

He nodded. "You're right."

The need to leave—to get as far away from Anya as he could manage—hit him with an urgency that sent him walking straight to his parka and jamming his arms inside its sleeves.

Anya didn't take so much as a step toward him. She stayed right where she was and watched him with a quiet determination that Brock felt like the snap of a cold, arctic wind.

Chapter Twelve

"I kissed Brock," Anya announced, rather unceremoniously, as she slid Clementine's latte across the counter.

Clementine didn't make a move to touch the latte, which only underscored the magnitude of Anya's predicament.

"You should probably take a sip. That mountain of whipped cream you requested is going to melt." Anya nodded toward the latte cup.

Clementine glanced at her drink and then back at Anya. "You can't just drop a bomb on me like that and expect me to dive into a pile of whipped cream."

Protestations aside, she dipped her finger into the whipped cream, scooping a generous portion of it into her mouth. "Mmmm. Okay, now that we've averted a whipped topping crisis, could you please enlighten me? Brock kissed you? When? Where?"

"No." Anya's neck grew hot. "*I* kissed *him*. Last night, at the cottage. It was an accident."

"An accident?" Clementine raised an eyebrow and reached for her latte. "How do you kiss someone by accident?"

"Okay, it wasn't an accident. I knew good and well what I was doing. But there were extenuating circumstances—*The Karate Kid*, a snowstorm and a breakthrough with Dolce. I couldn't help myself."

"*The Karate Kid*? Really?" Clementine smirked behind her latte cup. "We're in Alaska. There's a snowstorm every other day. I don't remember it ever being cause for you to go around kissing people."

"The point is, it was a mistake," Anya groaned. "A horrible mistake."

Clementine frowned and plunked her coffee on the counter. A few drops sloshed over the rim. "Really? A mistake? That surprises me. I've seen the way Brock looks at you. Was it really that awful?"

Awful? No. It was actually rather wonderful. More wonderful than I could have ever expected…

"Not that kind of mistake." Anya wiped the latte mess from the countertop and slipped her apron over her head.

The coffee bar wasn't even technically open, but Anya couldn't bring herself to face avalanche training with Brock this morning without a little emergency girl-talk session first. Although she hated to call Clementine at such an early hour, she knew the promise of a gourmet coffee drink would go a long way toward making it tolerable.

"Oh," Clementine said. "I see. You have feelings for him, don't you?"

Feelings for Brock? No, of course not. She'd just been caught up in the moment. That's all.

Yes, she was currently knitting a hat for the man in question. But that didn't necessarily mean anything either. She had to have something to occupy her time while she sat on the floor with Dolce.

"No," Anya said. She frowned when she realized how unconvincing she sounded. "Dolce walked out of the bedroom all on her own. I was elated. Brock was there, and I was…vulnerable."

"Vulnerable. I see." Clementine nodded.

Anya was grateful she refrained from pointing out that vulnerable people typically allowed themselves to be kissed rather than doing the actual kissing.

"I repeat—it was a mistake. Brock and I work together. I'm supposed to hide in a snow cave with him." She glanced at her watch. "In less than an hour. What should I do?"

"Personally, I think you'll end up regretting it if you decide not to go. You love volunteering with the ski patrol, and Brock will be leaving town soon anyway. Problem solved. But you have a choice. You don't have to do this."

Anya's thoughts turned at once to her Bible, sitting open on her night table. When Brock had left the night before—when she'd practically forced him out the door and into that snowstorm—and she couldn't make sense of what had happened, she'd sought clarity in God's word. Her Bible was still new enough that the spine cracked when she opened it. She hadn't really expected to find anything inside that would speak to her situation, but the book itself—the heaviness of it—was always a comfort.

She hadn't been quite sure what she was looking for. Something along the lines of *Blessed is she who kisses a handsome man by mistake* would have been nice. Of course she'd found nothing of the sort. Her eyes had landed on a verse right in the middle of the book of Isaiah, however, that gave her goose bumps.

Though the mountains be shaken and the hills be removed, yet my unfailing love for you will not be shaken.

Mountains that shook? Hills that gave way?

It had to be a sign. She was meant to help the avalanche search team. She knew it now with even greater certainty than she had before.

"Actually, I do." Anya squared her shoulders. "This is what God wants for me. I just know it."

Clementine sighed and polished off the last of her latte. "You really believe that, don't you?"

"Yes. I know it might sound crazy, but it feels right." As much as she believed she was following God's plan, there was still the awkward matter of the kiss to deal with. "The part I'm not so sure about is working side by side with Brock now."

"Anya, if working with the search team is really part of God's plan, you don't need to worry about the rest." Clementine gave her hand a gentle squeeze. "You just need to trust Him. It's His plan, not yours. The details are His to work out."

Could it really be that simple?

"You have a point," Anya said, letting Clementine's words sink in.

Kiss or no kiss, Brock was leaving. At least she knew about it in advance. She would just be more careful around him. He'd helped her so much with Dolce—his being in Aurora was certainly part of the plan. She could accept that. As Clementine had said, it wasn't her plan anyway. But Anya couldn't help but wonder exactly how much longer God intended for Brock to stick around—and how much easier things would be if He would consider sharing that information. She shook her head and reached for her parka. She needed to get going if she was going to make it to the ski mountain on time.

Clementine slid off her barstool and fell in step beside Anya as she headed toward the parking lot. "Maybe it's time to rethink your no-dating policy. You kissed Brock. That seems like a pretty good indication you're ready."

Must they talk about the kiss again?

"I told you. It was a mistake." Anya pulled her hat down lower over her ears.

The air had an extra bite to it as it sometimes did the morning after a snowstorm—colder and damper than usual. Swollen gray clouds filled the sky and hung so low that Anya imagined she could reach up and graze them with her fingertips. She shivered against the cold.

"Be careful up on the mountain." Clementine gave Anya a tight hug. "This weather makes me nervous."

Anya grinned as she headed for her car. "What kind of Alaskan would I be if I let a little snow scare me?"

She wasn't afraid of the snow or the cold or the eerie gray sky. What frightened her most was the thought of dating again.

Especially Brock Parker.

By the time the ski patrol was scheduled to begin its snow cave drills, Anya had begun to dream of snow. It came as no surprise, considering she'd spent more time in the snow over the course of the past few weeks than she had thus far in her entire life. This was quite a sweeping statement, given that she was Alaskan through and through. But accurate, nonetheless.

She'd hidden in holes, boxed in by snow on all sides. She'd rolled around playing with the dogs until snow filled her ears and drenched her hair. She'd even begun to ski again, finding her balance more quickly than she'd expected, given that she hadn't slipped her foot into a ski binding since Speed had left town. Sherlock would lie across her lap as they rode the chairlift to the top of the mountain. Then they would execute what Brock called a dog snow-plow to reach the training site—Anya would aim the front tips of her skis together, keeping the tails pushed wide apart so Sherlock could romp behind her legs. Once at the site, Anya and the others had dug more holes, trenches and snow caves than she could count.

And she'd loved every minute of it.

This was different from pouring coffee all day. When she was working with the dogs, Anya felt as though she'd found her place. She'd return to the coffee bar each day with her face glowing from the wind and the sheer excitement of it all and think-ing about things like scent cones and snow density while she mixed lattes.

Under Brock's tutelage, she and Sherlock had in-creased the level of their training by introducing a series of challenges. First, Cole held onto Sherlock for longer and longer periods while Anya ran and hid from view. When the dog passed that test with flying colors, still zipping right toward the trench to find Anya even after a five-minute waiting pe-riod, it was time for the hiding place to become more obscured.

The first time Anya had been buried in the trench, Brock had covered her with just a light dusting of snow—maybe an inch or two at most. He'd started with her feet, working his way up to her head. The last thing she'd seen before she closed her eyes was the smile on his face. It had lingered in her memory as the snow fell from his shovel and onto her cheeks, as soft and light as feathers.

Now as she trudged through the snow toward the ski patrol cabin, she was doing her best to forget about Brock's smile. And most of all, the kiss. She pledged to keep a degree of distance between the two of them before he left for good and that distance became even greater. And permanent.

So ten minutes later, when Anya found herself sitting less than an arm's length away from Brock in the confines of a tiny snow cave, she did her best to concentrate on her surroundings rather than on the company.

"I can't believe how warm it is in here." She peeled off one of her gloves and gingerly ran her fingertips along the ceiling, the wall, the packed snow floor. "Why is that?"

"It's not quite as warm as it seems. The temperature in here is probably around thirty-two degrees, although I suppose that's a good ten to fifteen degrees warmer than outside." Brock tugged off his black skullcap and ran his hand through his hair. "We're out of the wind. Plus, the cave itself retains heat."

Good to know. Anya had hoped there was some legitimate reason for the warmth coursing through her other than Brock's closeness. "How long do you think it will take Aspen and Jackson to find us?"

It was only the second day the dogs had begun working alongside their own handlers to find pretend avalanche victims and the first time the "victims" weren't hiding in plain sight.

Brock had decided it was best for the pretend victims to hide in pairs to saturate the area with scent. Before either of them could object, Cole announced he'd hide with Luke.

That left Brock and Anya. Together. In extremely close quarters. All around them, ice crystals glittered like diamonds in the snowy walls. Anya blinked against the romantic assault on her senses.

Brock appeared to consider her question and shrugged. "Who knows? They may find Cole and Luke first."

"True," she said. If that was the case, Cole would come and get them. Then it would be Anya's turn to search for victims with Sherlock. "Do you think Sherlock will be able to find someone in a cave? This seems much harder than searching for people in trenches."

Brock shook his head and smiled at his feet. He appeared to be as determined to avoid eye contact as she was. "If he were looking for you, he'd be able to do it in record speed. That dog is head over heels for you."

Anya's face grew a degree or two warmer. "I don't know about that."

"I do. But so far, it's worked out okay. He does whatever you ask. I only hope that he adapts this well to his permanent partner." He glanced at her ever so briefly. The inside of the snow cave was bathed in soft blue light, perfectly mirroring the color of his eyes.

She looked away. "I'm sure he will. He's a good dog."

"It doesn't always go so smoothly. Believe me." He frowned, and once again Anya caught a glimpse of the world weariness she'd seen in the fine lines of his face. This time, his expression told her he was more than just tired. She got the sense he carried a secret sadness somewhere deep inside.

She wanted to ask him about it. But she knew she had no right to ask questions of him, especially after pushing him away that memorable night. Why should she care anyway? It wasn't as if he was in her life to stay.

She needed to turn her attention to safer things. She looked around and saw nothing but snow on every side.

"I dreamed about the snow last night," she said.

"Did you?"

She nodded. "I dreamed I was alone under the

stars on a very dark night, swishing my arms and legs in the snow to make a snow angel. Isn't that funny? I haven't made a snow angel in years."

He replied with a small smile.

"You must dream of the snow all the time. Or have you been doing this so long it no longer fazes you?" She'd meant it as a casual question, just something to talk about until their "rescue."

But something in his expression gave her pause. He was unusually still, even for Brock. And when he turned his gaze on her, she found it impossible to look away.

His handsome features, so strong and chiseled, appeared to soften before her eyes. He seemed uncharacteristically vulnerable, a word she'd never before associated with Brock.

"I've dreamed of the snow every night for the past twenty-five years," he said in a way that made it clear those dreams didn't include snow angels.

"Oh?" Anya swallowed. She was suddenly very conscious of every breath she took, every subtle movement her body made in their close quarters. "That's a long time."

"Yes." He nodded, his jaw clenching. "Very long. Sometimes I don't think I'll ever dream of anything else."

She wondered if she should change the subject. Clearly, this wasn't a happy one. But she was intrigued with the idea of knowing him more. She'd told him so many things about her past, but she knew next to nothing of his. "Why, Brock?"

He sighed, breathing out a cloud of vapor that hung in the small space between them. "On a very snowy night when I was eight years old, my little brother went missing."

"Missing? Did he run away?" Anya held her breath and waited for an answer.

"No." Brock gave her a solemn look, and she knew what he would say even before the words left his lips. "He was taken."

A shiver ran up Anya's spine.

"Was he ever…" She gulped, unable to complete the question.

"No." He shook his head. "Never."

"How awful. I'm so sorry, Brock." She reached out and touched his arm.

He looked at her fingertips resting against the sleeve of his parka, then fixed his gaze on hers. Sadness seemed to pour from his blue eyes and settle inside her chest.

She had the distinct sensation she was somehow unlocking him, seeing a part of him no one had ever seen before. It made her feel as though her limbs were melting, becoming liquid, even though the temperature in the cave hovered close to freezing.

"This is why you do what you do, isn't it? Why you work so hard at search and rescue?" she asked.

"It was the snow. That night. It made it impossible

for the police to find clues the next day." His voice drifted somewhere between bitterness and grief. "It was everywhere. Inches and inches of it. I guess in a way, I declared war against the snow back then. I decided to go wherever it was worst and beat it. I'd hold it back with my bare hands if I could."

"And you're still fighting." Tears stung the backs of Anya's eyes as she realized what he was telling her. This was why he was leaving. He was fighting an adversary that could never be beaten.

"I can't stop." His eyes were practically pleading, as if she could tell him how to give up the fight. As if she held all the answers.

It was both humbling and stirring. "You can't keep fighting an unbeatable enemy. No matter where you go, no matter how many people you save, you can't bring back your brother. Aren't you tired? I don't know much about God, Brock. But I do know He can help you. Don't you just sometimes want to let it all go?"

"No. Never."

She swallowed. So this was the truth about Brock—his past had turned him into a tragic hero.

"I've never even been tempted to let it go…" He cupped her cheek in his hand. His fingertips were surprisingly warm against her skin. "…until now."

With his touch, the air in the tiny cave seemed to sparkle just as brightly and beautifully as the icy crystals that surrounded them. Anya lifted her gaze to his and looked right into his eyes—the exact shade of blue as a glacier—and could see he was telling the truth.

She wished it were possible to freeze time as easily as it was to freeze water, for the air to grow cold and change rain to sleet. Because if it were, she would freeze this moment—stay right here in the snow cave with Brock looking at her the way he was now.

As though he wanted to kiss her.

"Brock," she whispered, unsure of what exactly she wanted to say. She just wanted to hear his name on her lips. Now, while he was still here.

"Shh," he murmured, then leaned closer as if to silence her with the touch of his lips.

A shiver ran up Anya's spine, a shiver that would have found her regardless of whether they'd been in a snow cave or on a tropical island somewhere basking under a warm summer sun. Brock's thumb moved in a slow, deliberate circle, caressing her cheek, and he lifted her face so it was aligned perfectly with his.

There was a delicious moment of anticipation as she let her eyes drift closed and waited for their lips to meet, then a voice broke though the sweet silence.

It was distinctly nontender. And very much non-Brock. "Hey, you two."

Anya's eyes flew open, and she spotted Cole crawling on his belly, entering the cave. His eyebrows were crusted with frost, and a fine layer of snow tipped the edges of his eyelashes.

At the sudden sight of Cole, Brock backed away from her so fast that he bumped his head on the cave wall behind him. "Ouch."

"You okay?" Cole eyed him with concern.

When Brock merely nodded, Cole aimed a curious glance back and forth between the two of them. "Is everything all right in here?"

"Yes." Anya pasted on a smile.

Brock cleared his throat. "Of course."

If Cole found it odd that the two of them were so quick to respond or that they now avoided looking at one another with a dogged determination, he didn't give any indication. "Good. You can come on out now. Aspen alerted where Luke and I were hiding."

"Great," Brock said.

Was it her imagination, or did his voice sound oddly detached? What did that mean? What did any of this mean?

It didn't matter. This wasn't the time or place to ask Brock why he'd almost kissed her. She had a job to do and Cole was right there waiting for her to do it.

Even so, her thoughts were far from the task at hand. They dwelled instead on Brock's past, on a little boy waking up one snowy morning to find his brother gone.

How does someone move past something so painful, even after all these years?

"So Aspen found you. Super." It was a valiant struggle to keep any traces of emotion out of her voice. "Sherlock and I are up now, right?"

"Yep." Cole worked his way backward until he'd shimmied out of the cave.

When Cole offered her his hand to help her up and out, she hesitated.

"Brock?" Anya glanced over her shoulder at him, but the vulnerable man she'd glimpsed only moments before was gone. His features were blank—rather stern, actually. Once again, he resembled the picture-perfect hero she'd found looking back at her from all those photos she'd seen on the Internet. And just like before, his blue eyes were focused on her forehead.

"You should go up." He pulled on his black knit hat and scooped Anya's gloves off the cave floor.

"Okay," she said around the lump in her throat.

She reached for her gloves. His fingertips grazed hers when she took them from him, and she couldn't help but notice that the warmth was gone from his hands.

They were as cold as ice.

Chapter Thirteen

"Sherlock, come." Brock stood ten or twelve feet away from the dog, an all but insignificant distance in the world of search and rescue training, and called Sherlock. Again. And again the dog ignored him.

Brock took a few steps closer and tried the command once more. The results were the same. This time, as if to put a punctuation mark on his disobedience, Sherlock plopped down on his belly in the snow and rested his chin on his outstretched legs.

Then the dog had the audacity to close his eyes.

"Giving me the silent treatment today?" Brock sighed.

He could appreciate the irony of the situation. Sherlock was treating Brock in the same manner in which Brock had been treating Anya since the near-kiss in the snow cave. Being on the receiving end of such behavior wasn't at all pleasant, he noted.

Not that everything had been all sunshine and roses on his end either. Simply put, he was miserable.

Brock had carefully arranged his schedule over the past week so that his training schedule overlapped with Anya's as little as possible. This morning, he'd dragged Sherlock to the mountain just so they could work on recalls while Anya was away. Brock now worked with the dogs one on one when she was at the coffee bar, and during those times she was present at the ski resort, he avoided being alone with her at all costs. Because apparently, he could no longer be trusted to behave in a professional manner.

Not that avoiding someone was altogether professional.

In truth, Brock was beyond the point of worrying about professionalism. Out of necessity, he'd switched to personal protection mode. He'd crossed a line when he'd told Anya about his past. Now there was no going back, but he was incapable of moving forward.

So that left him where, exactly?

Missing her, he mused, as Sherlock let loose with a snore loud enough to start an avalanche.

"Bud, wake up. You're not getting off that easy." Brock gave Sherlock a gentle nudge with the toe of his hiking boot.

The dog begrudgingly got to his feet.

"Let's try this one more time." Brock ran a hand over Sherlock's head.

The dog peered up at him. For a moment, Brock imagined he could see a profound wisdom in Sherlock's eyes. The soft gold of his irises seemed to hold all of Brock's secrets, as though Sherlock knew precisely why Brock was acting the way he was toward Anya. Knew and clearly didn't approve.

A voice broke out in the stillness of the mountainside. "Having trouble with Sherlock again?"

Brock turned to find Jackson walking toward him, with Aspen bounding alongside. When Aspen saw Brock, he broke away from Jackson's side. The dog romped toward Brock, then back again, as if torn between two masters. Normal behavior for a pup still in training. As far at the other end of the spectrum from Sherlock's deliberate moodiness as it got.

Brock hung his head in frustration. "You could say that."

"Sorry. Let me know if I can help." Jackson glanced at Sherlock, and the dog wagged his tail.

"Thanks," Brock said, knowing even as he did that he wouldn't take Jackson up on his offer. He knew instinctively that it wouldn't help.

"If I didn't know better, I'd say Sherlock is mad at you." Jackson frowned. "He doesn't even want to look at you."

"I've noticed."

Jackson raised his brows. "Not to pry, but is Cole mad at you too?"

Brock's gaze darted immediately to Jackson. "What? Why would you think that?"

"Just something Cole said." He shrugged. "Don't worry about it. It's probably nothing. I'm sorry I asked. I'm sure if there was a problem, you'd know about it."

There was indeed a problem. Multiple ones, in fact. Brock just hadn't realized Cole was privy to that illustrious list. Brock's mess of a relationship with Anya ranked as number one, followed by Sherlock's naughty streak.

"What exactly did Cole say?" Maybe if he could narrow things down, Brock could begin to repair whatever damage had been done.

Right. Look what happened last time you tried to fix things with Anya—you ended up kissing her.

Technically, she'd kissed him. But it didn't matter. If she hadn't made the first move, he would have done so himself. He knew that now.

"Cole just said you two needed to talk. That's all." Jackson pulled a tug toy out of his parka and Sherlock sprung to his feet, ready to play. "It's probably nothing."

"I'm sure you're right," Brock said, even though deep down he wasn't sure at all.

He wasn't sure of anything anymore.

* * *

We need to talk.

Brock figured it had to be one of the most dreaded phrases in the English language. And here he was, on the receiving end of it.

"We need to talk," Cole said, sounding uncharacteristically business-like from the other end of the phone line, although Brock could have been imagining the sudden change in his demeanor. Was there a nonthreatening way in which to issue such a statement? If so, he'd never heard it.

"Okay." Brock reached for Sherlock and gave him a good rub between the ears, usually a gesture meant to reassure the dog. Funny how it worked the other way around too.

"Can you come in early today? There are some things we need to discuss."

Brock glanced at his Swiss Army watch. There were still no clocks in the house he'd rented for his duration in Aurora. They fell into the category of items he usually didn't bother to unpack. "Sure. Do you want me to head over?"

"That would be great. See you soon." Cole hung up.

Brock shoved his cell phone in his pocket and reached for his parka. "Come on, boys. No rest for the weary."

Sherlock and Aspen sprung to their feet, and he couldn't help but laugh. Those two were hardly weary. They didn't know the meaning of the word. Four straight hours of training last night on the mountain, and they were already anxious to give it another go.

They'd make great rescue dogs. Aspen would anyway. Sherlock was still far too attached to Anya for Brock to have any idea how he would adjust to working with his permanent handler. And this business about him refusing to obey Brock just wasn't acceptable. Perhaps Cole had gotten wind of the situation, and that's why he'd summoned Brock to the patrol headquarters.

We need to talk.

The words haunted him as he snapped leashes on Sherlock and Aspen's harnesses and loaded them into the truck. His temples throbbed. Hadn't he done enough talking lately?

He'd certainly done a lot of talking the week before when he'd been hiding in the snow cave with Anya. He'd told her things he'd never before shared with anyone. In all the years he'd been traveling the world, Brock had never once explained to another living soul why he did it.

Brock wished he could blame his sudden frankness with Anya on some sort of idea of reciprocity. She'd shared her past with him, so naturally he'd wanted to share his with her. But deep down, he knew reciprocity had nothing to do with why he'd told her about his brother.

He'd wanted to tell her. *Everything.* Including how for the first time in his life, he was tempted to stop. To just stay right where he was and breathe in the cold Alaskan air day after day. For the rest of his life. As if telling her such things could somehow make them possible.

Brock knew better. He and Anya may have been protected from the outside world while they'd hidden behind the crystal walls of that snow cave, but the past always had a way of finding him. There was nowhere he could hide.

As he drove past Aurora Community Church on the way to the ski mountain, he remembered what Anya had said about God.

He can help you.

But could He? Could He really?

Brock wasn't so sure. Where had God been that night when Drew disappeared? And where had He been in the tortured years since?

His gaze was drawn toward the building's tall white steeple like a magnet. He tried to remember the last time he'd been in a church. About a year and a half ago he'd spent three solid days living out of an old-world cathedral high atop a mountain in the Italian Alps. The cathedral had opened its doors and become the headquarters for the avalanche search team he'd helicoptered in with after a deadly slide in the area. Brock had slept—or tried to sleep—each of the three nights on a pew. He could remember lying there, his body and spirit both weary from days of searching for survivors he'd ultimately never found, staring up at the moonbeams shining through the stained glass windows in sapphire shafts of light. Despite the failure pressing down on him from an unsuccessful search, he'd felt a sudden stillness come over him. It didn't make any sense at all, but in that moment he'd experienced the closest thing to peace that he'd known since he was a kid, since before Drew had disappeared.

Still, Brock didn't suppose that incident really counted. He hadn't heard any sort of sermon, hadn't uttered a word of prayer. He'd done nothing but eat, sleep and care for the search dogs in that holy building—and even then, only when darkness and weather conditions rendered rescue attempts impossible.

Brock pressed on the accelerator and refocused on the matter at hand as the church vanished from his rearview mirror.

We need to talk.

Brock had a feeling he knew exactly what Cole wanted to talk about, and it wasn't Sherlock's rebellious streak.

It was Anya.

Brock had very nearly kissed her. *During a training exercise.* What had he been thinking? And since then he'd avoided her like the plague. He was certain the situation hadn't escaped Cole's notice.

As Brock pulled his truck into the small lot at the base of the mountain, he couldn't help but wonder how much Cole had seen when he'd crawled into the snow cave. He slammed the truck into park and realized it didn't matter what Cole had seen. The air had been so thick with emotion, anyone could have felt it. Cole must have known he'd stumbled onto something. Something Brock had no business pursuing.

When he walked into the cabin and saw Anya sitting across the worn wooden table from Cole, he knew without a doubt that his suspicions were right. This conference was definitely about the two of them.

The pain in Brock's temples intensified. He could understand Cole being upset with him, but was it really necessary to force Anya to sit through this meeting? The fault rested entirely on his shoulders. She didn't deserve this.

Brock did his best to send her a silent apology with his eyes, but his efforts were lost in the frenzy that ensued when Sherlock spotted Anya. The dog lunged straight toward her in a blur of unbridled, tail-wagging affection. Before Brock could utter a command, Anya had Sherlock situated in a calm sitting position at her feet.

Cole shook his head and laughed. "That dog would walk over hot coals for you."

"Hot coals? I'm not so sure about that," Anya said with a self-deprecating smile tipping her lips. "But he's a good boy. Aren't you, Sherlock? That's right. You're a good boy."

Sherlock's tail thumped on the hardwood floor with enough enthusiasm to rock the cabin. Despite the nagging sense of dread in Brock's gut about the purpose of the meeting, he smiled. He gave Aspen a hearty scratch behind the ears so he wouldn't feel left out of the excitement and then sank into the seat halfway between Anya and Cole.

Cole wasted no time getting right down to business. "I'd like to thank the two of you for coming in so early this morning. I can't help but think you both have a good idea why I've called you here."

Brock's gut twisted. Of course he knew why he was here. That didn't mean he was happy about it. He cast another apologetic glance at Anya, but her gaze was fixed directly on Cole.

"I've been giving our situation quite a bit of thought." Cole paused.

So things had progressed to a *situation*.

Great. Just great.

Cole folded his hands in front of him. "The way I see it, there's only one solution."

Brock braced himself. Either he was about to be fired for the first time in his career, or Anya was being dumped from the training team. If it was the former, at least he knew he had a job waiting for him in Utah. Guy Wallace had been relentless, leaving voicemails on his phone every two or three days.

If it was the latter and Anya was the one being given walking papers, Brock and Cole would be having words.

Cole took a deep, audible breath. Then he smiled, which Brock found odd. "Anya…"

Beneath the table, Brock's fists clenched.

"…you've really impressed me with the work you've done with Sherlock thus far. As you know, it's been my hope that Brock would agree to stay on here in Aurora and run our search dog program. It doesn't look like he's ready to make that kind of commitment."

Brock's fists clenched tighter. Where was Cole going with this? It suddenly didn't appear as though anyone would be let go, but Brock nevertheless felt distinctly uncomfortable with the discussion.

Was it really necessary to bring attention to his lack of "commitment"? Hearing Cole's words through Anya's ears made Brock cringe.

Cole's gaze flitted from Anya to Brock. "To that end, I've decided the best thing might be to make Anya an official, full-time, paid member of the Aurora Ski Patrol Unit. If she's interested, that is. What do you think, Brock?"

It was the last thing Brock had expected, although he wasn't sure why. Now that Cole had made the suggestion, it seemed like the obvious solution.

Still, something within him railed against the idea. How could it be that Anya—the one woman who'd ever made him wish he could let go of the past and build a life, a real life, with someone—would end up being the one person who could make his departure possible? If this were to happen, if Anya were to become Sherlock's handler, the ski patrol's problems would be solved, for the most part. For all intents and purposes, she would be his ticket out of Aurora. He could leave as planned and not suffer a moment's worry about the avalanche search dog program he was leaving behind.

It was the cruelest of ironies.

Not to mention the fact that if Anya was a member of the avalanche search team, he would be leaving her in harm's way. She wouldn't just be training the dogs, practicing for a potential disaster. She'd be right there in the center of things.

"Brock?" Cole raised his brows. "How about it? Don't you think Anya would be a perfect addition to the team?"

Yes. Brock swallowed. *Yes, she would. Just say it.*

Anya gazed up at him, her violet eyes wide with hope and expectation. Brock wondered what those eyes would look like a year, five years, a decade from now, after she'd pulled her share of lifeless bodies from underneath the hard-packed snow of a slide.

He looked away.

He couldn't do it. Maybe it made him her hero. Maybe it made him a coward. Either way, he wouldn't be the one who took that innocent sparkle from her eyes.

In as calm a voice as he could manage, he said, "I'm not so sure that's a good idea."

Anya couldn't possibly have heard Brock correctly. "Excuse me?"

Brock hadn't so much as spoken to her since their encounter in the snow cave. Anya didn't know what to make of it. One minute he was leaning in to kiss her, and the next he was pretending as though she didn't exist. And now he was telling Cole she shouldn't be a part of the ski patrol.

He cleared his throat. "I said I'm not sure if making you an official member of the ski patrol is the best idea."

"Of course it's not the *best* idea. As Cole just said, the *best* idea would be if you agreed to stay on." She swallowed. "But you've made it clear that's not an option."

Brock's gaze dropped to the table. For a moment, Anya felt guilty about reiterating the fact that Cole's first choice for the job was Brock himself. Now that she knew about the disappearance of Brock's brother, she could understand that things were more complicated than she'd initially thought. Even after all she'd been through, she couldn't quite bring herself to feel betrayed by the fact that he was leaving.

But she *could* feel betrayed by Brock's reaction to Cole offering her a real job on the team.

It was one thing to go about his business, ignoring her as though they'd never shared a moment of tenderness. But it was another thing entirely for him to try to steal this opportunity from her. How dare he?

"You don't think I can do it, do you?"

Brock leveled his gaze at her once again. "That's not at all what I said."

Cole intervened. "Let's all slow down for a minute."

His gaze swiveled back and forth between the two of them before finally resting on Brock. "I must say, Brock, I'm surprised. Making Anya an official part of the team seems like the obvious solution. I assumed you'd be on board one hundred percent. You said yourself she's a natural."

He'd said that? About her?

She searched his expression and could tell it was true by the softening of his chiseled features.

"Yes." He nodded. "Yes, I did."

Anya's anger ebbed somewhat. Just a bit. She was reminded of what he'd told her in the snow cave—about how she possessed a gift for the work they were doing. Those words had settled in her soul with a sweetness she could almost taste, like honey. No one had ever said anything of the sort to her before. She knew full well she could make a great cup of coffee, but this…this was different.

"Then what's the problem?" she asked, her voice growing wobbly. "I don't understand."

She bit the inside of her cheek. She would *not* cry. Not here in front of Brock and Cole. When she got back home to the cottage, she could cry all she wanted. She could wrap her arms around Dolce—who'd at last progressed to spending all her time right on Anya's heels—and sob her heart out. But she would not do so here. She wasn't about to give Cole any more reason to question her suitability for the job.

Brock took a long, slow inhale. "Training the dogs is one thing. Doing the work itself is another entirely. There are many other facets to avalanche rescue work besides dog handling."

Anya lifted her brows. "Such as?"

"You'd need helo training," he said cryptically, as if trying to use lingo she was unfamiliar with on purpose.

The joke was on him. She knew exactly what it meant. "I've ridden my fair share of helicopters. I live in small-town Alaska, remember? Small aircraft transportation is more common here than riding in a car."

"She has a point," Cole said. Anya got the distinct impression he was stifling a grin.

"What else?" she asked, focusing all her attention once again on Brock.

"Well…probe poles. You'd need to learn how to

use probe poles." He crossed his arms and settled back in his chair.

Was he just looking for excuses? Anya was well aware of what a probe pole was. She'd seen groups of them lined up along the wall in Brock's barn back on that very first day. The day of the bear suit, as she'd come to think of it. She'd even Googled their use back when Brock was still Mr. Miyagi-ing her on a daily basis.

Brock, of course, didn't know this. Well, he would now. "I think I understand the theory behind probing—doesn't common sense dictate you'd start at the bottom of the slide and work your way up?"

At this, Cole laughed. "I knew this was a good idea. She's done her homework, Brock. There's no denying it."

Brock's eyes flashed. He leaned forward, resting his elbows on the table, and pinned her with a grim look. "You've done your homework? Then surely you know the only options searchers possess for locating avalanche victims are dog teams, pole teams and beacons?"

"Yes." She lifted her chin.

Of course she knew about beacons. Brock never let her set foot on the mountain unless she was armed with one. In the event of a slide, its signal could be activated at once, letting rescuers know her exact location. Skiers on avalanche-prone slopes were encouraged to carry beacons at all times.

Brock's gaze bored into her, unrelenting. "And I suppose you also know that the first fifteen minutes are the most crucial for locating victims?"

She nodded.

He angled his head toward her. "Remind me why that is, if you would."

Her heart clenched ever so slightly as she began to realize what he was getting at.

"The sooner the victim is found, the more likely they are to survive," she answered softly.

Brock wasn't finished making his point. "The survival rate for an avalanche victim drops to a mere thirty percent at the thirty-five-minute mark. Did you know that?"

She hadn't known that. Not exactly. She knew that the longer a person was buried, the more dangerous the situation became. But she hadn't thought enough about it to put exact numbers on the odds. Now that Brock did, she began to realize how daunting they actually were.

"After thirty-five minutes, the odds drop rather drastically." Brock turned his attention to Cole. "She needs to understand that searches—real searches—don't always end successfully like they do in training. Before you ask her to make a decision about her future, you owe it to her to make sure she understands that someday Sherlock will be helping her uncover a body under the snow. A dead body."

Brock pushed out of his chair and began to pace

around the small cabin. In a move that spoke of pure frustration, he jammed a hand through his hair, tugging on the ends. He looked more like a Viking than ever before—cold, stony, like he was ready to go to battle.

So he was frustrated. Fine. He wasn't the only one.

"I'd appreciate it if you wouldn't talk about me like I'm not even in the room. I'm sitting right here." She slammed her hand on the table for added emphasis.

Brock cast Anya a tortured glance that told her he was well aware of her presence. As if he felt her nearness down to the marrow of his bones, the way she always did around him.

She blinked. Of course he didn't. That was absurd. He wasn't even speaking to her.

Cole cleared his throat. "Perhaps we should all sleep on this for a night or two. Anya, the offer stands. Let me know when you've had a chance to think it over."

"I don't need to sleep on it," she said to Cole and Cole alone. "I'd love to be a part of your team."

"Okay then. We'll be lucky to have you." Cole winced. "Oh boy, half the town will be after my head once they hear you're leaving the coffee bar."

Anya laughed. She wished Brock would laugh with her. Or at the very least crack a smile.

He didn't. He crossed his arms and looked down

at her with a sadness in his gaze that reached into her chest and squeezed like a vise.

"Congratulations," he said with a bittersweet smile.

And for a moment—a sweet, naïve moment—Anya thought that was the end of it, that everything would go on as it had before, that the two of them would somehow find the tenderness they'd lost over the course of the past few days.

She couldn't have been more wrong.

Brock turned to Cole. "I suppose this clears the way then."

Clears the way? What was he talking about?

Cole nodded. "If you say so. As you mentioned, there's still quite a bit of training to do. How much time do you think we need?"

Brock glanced at Sherlock and Aspen. Both dogs were curled on the floor sound asleep, oblivious to all that had just transpired. "A few weeks. Two, maybe three?"

Dread pooled in the pit of Anya's belly. Surely he didn't mean what she thought he meant. It was too unexpected, too soon.

"Very well, then." Cole rose, walked to the desk beneath the window overlooking the ski mountain and jotted something down on a legal pad. "I have your exit date marked down as three weeks from today."

Exit date?

Exit date!

Anya was panicked to her core. She didn't dare try to speak or stand, afraid she would say the wrong thing or break down like she had at the Reindeer Run. She concentrated all her efforts on keeping herself together. Once she could breathe without consciously reminding herself to do so, she lifted her gaze to Brock and found him watching her with an earnestness that felt as if it might tear her in two.

He turned to go. Both dogs scrambled to their feet and followed him to the door. As Anya watched him go, a lump rose to her throat. She couldn't help but wonder if the real reason he'd been so reluctant to name her as Sherlock's permanent handler was that he knew such a change would pave the way for his departure. Did the idea of his leaving strike him straight in the heart as it did her?

Deep down she knew it didn't, no matter how badly she wished it were so. Brock had always known he'd leave. Even if he was tempted to stay, as he'd confessed to her in the snow cave, he wouldn't.

Or couldn't.

Either way, in a matter of weeks he'd be gone forever.

Chapter Fourteen

"There's a head poking out of your backpack," Anya's mother said as she stood in the doorway and frowned.

Anya paused on the threshold. It wasn't as if she could take a step inside the house with her mother guarding the entrance like that. She swallowed a sigh. She'd still harbored the desperate hope that today wouldn't be as stressful as she'd imagined. The crew from church was due to arrive in fifteen minutes. Surely her mother wasn't planning on standing guard like that all morning.

"This is Dolce." Anya slid the backpack from her shoulders. "She's my dog—the one I rescued. Remember?"

Her mother's lips turned up in a slight smile. The wary look still lingered in her eyes, but Anya was grateful for the shift in her demeanor, no matter how subtle. "This is the shy little thing you told me about?"

"Yes." Dolce's eyes darted between Anya and her mother, but she kept her head exposed. The first few times Anya had carried her out and about in the backpack, the little dog had ducked down inside like a baby kangaroo.

Baby steps. "She's really come a long way in the past month or so."

Her mother's expression softened a bit more. "Why are you carrying her in a bag like that? Can't she walk?"

"Yes, she can. But she's still quite timid. She feels safe in the backpack, though. This way she can still go places with me. It helps with her socialization."

"Socialization?" Anya's mom shook her head and rolled her eyes, as though it were a foreign language.

Good grief. She'd sounded just like Brock, hadn't she? What was next? Romping around town in a bear suit?

Absolutely not. Brock might be brilliant. And he might look surprisingly cute in the shaggy thing, but Anya doubted she could pull it off with the same panache. Besides, she might be his protégée, but she had to draw the line somewhere.

"Why don't we go inside? It's freezing out here." Anya nodded over her mother's shoulder toward the living room.

With a touch of reluctance, she opened the door wider. "I suppose all your friends are going to want to come inside, too?"

"They're coming here to work, Mom. On the roof, and out in the yard shoveling snow. No one's going to force their way inside. I brought along a big box of coffee to share, though." She set the coffee and a stack of paper cups from the Northern Lights Inn on the butcher block counter separating the kitchen from the living room. "It wouldn't kill you to invite them in. They're here to help, remember?"

Her mother glared at the box of coffee. "I knew they would expect something in return."

As if the worth of a cup of coffee was roughly equal to deicing someone's roof. Ridiculous.

"That's not what this is about." It was a struggle to keep her voice even. Why did she bother? Maybe she should have taken her mother at her word and stayed out of it—just let the roof cave right in. Would that have really been better than accepting help from a handful of well-meaning strangers?

Her mother peeled back the lace curtain from one of the living room windows and peeked outside. Anya sank onto the sofa and cradled Dolce in her lap, backpack and all. She ran her hand over Dolce's petite head and was struck with the realization that, odd as it might seem, her dog and her mother had a few things in common. Both had been hurt in the past. Through circumstances out of their control, both of them had become distrustful of people. Her mother all but hid inside her house much the way Dolce had hid under the bed for almost a year.

It was a sobering comparison. After all, one of them was a dog and the other a person. Not just any person, but her mother. And while her mother certainly had her share of faults, she'd always been there for Anya—which was far more than could be said of her father. But Anya was suddenly very aware that she had a choice to make.

"Here they come." Her mother rearranged the curtain back into place, crossed her arms and promptly uncrossed them. "Why don't you answer the door?"

Anya suppressed a smile as she realized her mother wasn't upset about the volunteers coming to help out. She was nervous. As nervous as Dolce had been when Anya first brought her home. It would have been cute if it weren't so sad.

As Anya rose to answer the door, she wondered about the choices she'd made in the years since Speed had left. Was she destined to end up like her mother? Or even Dolce? Had her efforts at self-preservation meant that she'd been living her life under the bed, as it were?

And if Dolce could start over after all she'd been through, did that mean Anya could too? Or would she wait until she was her mother's age to finally let someone in?

Her father had left. Speed had left. And now Brock was leaving. His departure date loomed over her like a black cloud heavy with snow—not the kind of snow that blanketed everything in a charming layer of glistening white, but the kind that thickened the air, making it impossible to see or breathe. But in the end, Anya would still have a life to live. Even after he was gone.

She opened the door and found Zoey standing on the other side, along with a few other people she recognized. Among them was Cole, who waved at her as he went to work pulling a ladder out of the bed of someone's pickup truck.

Zoey greeted her with a broad smile. "Good morning."

"Morning." Anya swung the door open wider. "Thank you so much for bringing all this help. Come on in."

"Did you know you have a dog in your backpack?" Zoey's eyes danced as she peered over Anya's shoulder and stepped inside. "Is that Dolce, your dog I've heard so much about?"

"Yes, this is Dolce." Anya's voice was laced with pride.

"She's so cute! Can I pet her?"

"Yes, but move really slowly. She's still very timid around new people and places."

Anya watched and murmured words of encouragement to Dolce as Zoey ran gentle fingers over the dog's little muzzle. Dolce responded with a tiny wag of her tail, a movement so subtle Anya scarcely felt it through the padding of her backpack. *More baby steps.*

"Would you like to come in for a cup of coffee?" Anya asked.

"Sure. Thank you." Zoey stomped the snow from her feet and stepped inside, giving Dolce a wide berth, a thoughtful gesture that made Anya smile.

Anya introduced Zoey to her mother and went to pour her a cup of coffee. And it was amazing—Zoey managed to engage her mom in conversation. They were talking to one another—far less awkwardly than Anya would have imagined—when the doorbell rang.

"That's probably a few more members of our team. We're expecting another pair of hands." Zoey searched for a spot to set down her cup.

"Finish your coffee. I'll get the door." Anya crossed the room and swung the door open, expecting to find another familiar face on the other side.

She did. Only this particular familiar face belonged to the last person she ever dreamed she'd see standing on her mother's front porch.

"Brock?" She was so confused and disoriented at the sight of him that she couldn't think of a thing to say.

Brock appeared equally surprised by the turn of events. He stared at her for a few silent, awkward seconds before finally speaking. "Anya? What are you doing here?"

"I grew up here. This is my mom's house. What are you doing here?"

"Cole asked me to come. Actually, he pretty much begged. I don't know why I agreed. The last time he asked me to show up somewhere mysterious, I ended up in danger of being gored by a reindeer." He frowned. "I had no idea you'd be here."

Anya had to force herself to smile. For the briefest moment she'd somehow convinced herself Brock had had a change of heart—that he'd come looking for her to tell her he wasn't leaving after all. That he was staying. For her.

How could she have been so foolish? And so wrong?

She was mortified. She almost wished she could dive under the nearest bed, Dolce-style.

Get yourself together.

"Cole is up on the roof." She pointed toward the ceiling. "With the others."

"I should probably head on up there," he mumbled in such a low tone she almost didn't hear.

He'd barely turned to go when his gaze wandered to Anya's backpack. "Now there's a familiar face I'm happy to see."

He gave Dolce a grin as big as Alaska itself. Anya's stomach fluttered. And her heart. Pretty much all her insides took flight when he smiled like that.

"I've begun carrying her around with me." Anya shrugged. "You know…socialization and all that."

"I'm familiar with the concept." His smile grew

broader, and she felt as though she might float right out of her shoes.

This had to stop. It really did.

She opened her mouth, prepared to send Brock outside to climb up on the roof, shovel snow or perform some other manly task for which he was so perfectly suited. But instead, she found herself saying, "Come inside for a bit?"

He lingered in the doorway with a barely discernible look of longing in his eyes. Then he took a step toward her. Just a step. Anya held her breath as he stood there, suspended between two worlds. Then some unseen force seemed to stop him.

"I think I'll just head on out and give Cole a hand." He nodded, and before Anya even realized what had happened, he was gone.

It was the closest they'd come to having any sort of real interaction since that day in the snow cave. And it had lasted less than a minute.

An hour later Brock had shed his parka, hat, gloves and scarf. And he was still sweating. He'd shoveled a path through shoulder-deep snow in Anya's mother's backyard and picked away at enough ice on the roof to make a hockey rink.

Not that he was complaining.

He'd needed an outlet for the frustration that had found its way into his muscles when he'd realized he'd been set up.

Cole had acted so nonchalant when he'd asked Brock to come help him out with a church project. He'd never once mentioned they'd be working on the house where Anya grew up.

Brock sighed and heaved another shovelful of snow off the edge of the roof. So Cole *had* noticed the sparks bouncing off the walls of the snow cave when he'd crawled inside. It was the only explanation. He'd suspected there was something going on between Brock and Anya, and now he wanted to play matchmaker.

Well, it wasn't going to work.

"Brock," Cole panted. "Let's take a break."

"A break?"

"Yes, a break. We're just about done here. We've been at this for more than two hours." Cole handed off his hammer and chisel to one of his fellow church members.

Two hours? Had that much time passed already?

"Okay. I'll see you down below." Brock speared his shovel into the snow, wiped his hands on his coveralls and shimmied down the ladder.

A group of folks stood sipping coffee on the porch, but Brock didn't have it in him to socialize. Coffee sounded good, though—Anya's coffee, in particular.

He headed inside, where he'd seen the cardboard box emblazoned with the insignia from the Northern Lights Inn's coffee bar. He was relieved to find the living room empty, save for a few people headed back out to the porch. And Anya.

She smiled at him as he approached. "Do you need to warm up? It's awfully cold out there today."

He was already warm. Even more so now that he was in her presence again. "Actually, I'd love some coffee."

"Sure." She began pouring him a cup, even though that wasn't his intention.

This wasn't the coffee bar. He didn't expect her to wait on him. "I can get that."

"I've got it. No problem." She held a full cup toward him.

"Thank you," he said and took a sip.

It was outlandishly good, even better than he'd remembered. Cole was right. The whole town would probably rise up in protest once they found out Anya would be leaving the coffee business to join the search and rescue team.

"Have you told anyone yet?" he asked.

"Told anyone?" She tilted her head, and a lock of silky hair fell across her cheek.

Brock's fingers itched to reach out and smooth it back into place. He tightened his grip on his paper coffee cup and shoved his free hand in one of his pockets. "About joining the unit."

"I told Zoey and my boss at the hotel. But I still need to tell my mom." She bit her lip, drawing his attention at once to her mouth.

He looked pointedly away.

This was insane. He was going to have to start focusing on her forehead again. He glanced at it and frowned. It was no use. Even her forehead was beautiful.

"Where is your mom?"

"In her sewing room. She's not exactly social." Anya released a sigh.

The frustration behind it reminded Brock of how upset she'd appeared that night back at her cottage after she'd visited her mother. Apparently, that hadn't been a one-time thing. "You and your mom don't see eye to eye about things, do you?"

"I guess you could say that. Sometimes I wish we were closer, but there's a lot of history there."

Brock understood all about that. His own family thought his lifestyle was insane. He often wondered if they were right, especially lately. "I didn't realize you were native Alaskan."

"No? I can't imagine why. Look at me—fair skin and these ridiculous eyes." She waved a hand toward her face.

His jaw clenched. "Your eyes are far from ridiculous. Don't ever think that."

"Oh." Her cheeks glowed pink. "Well, thank you."

Brock said nothing. He'd already said too much.

"Anyway," she continued. "I'm Russian, but I don't feel Russian at all. I grew up looking nothing like any of the family I knew. I suppose I shouldn't be surprised that the differences didn't end there."

He wished he could tell her just how lovely she was. The words were right there on the tip his tongue. "How do you think she'll feel about your new job?"

"Oh, I don't know." Anya shrugged. "I hope she won't worry too much. She's a worrier."

"For the record, I think it's great."

She peered up at him through her eyelashes and smiled—a slow, modest lift of her lips. "You do?"

"Yes. I know my initial reaction to the news probably wasn't what you'd expected." The more he thought about it, the more ashamed he was. He'd acted like a jerk. "I'm sorry."

"Apology accepted," she said, and whatever remaining awkwardness there had been between them slipped away.

Without thinking, Brock slipped his hand from his pocket and touched her face—just a light sweep of his fingertips across the soft skin of her cheek. "You'll be wonderful. Just the right woman for the job."

"Job?"

At the unexpected interruption, Brock jerked his hand back.

He tore his gaze from Anya and found her mother standing on the periphery. He'd been so wrapped up in Anya—her eyes, her words, the new part of her that she'd begun to share with him—that he'd been blindly unaware of anything else.

"What's this about a job?" Anya's mother furrowed her brow.

"A new job, yes," Anya stammered. "I'm leaving the coffee bar."

"What?" Her mother aimed a brief, accusatory look at Brock. "Why?"

Brock took a step backward.

"I'm joining the ski patrol. I'm going to work full time with the avalanche search dogs," Anya said, her head swiveling back and forth between Brock and her mother. "Mom, this is Brock. He's…"

She seemed confused as to how to introduce him, how to explain his role in her life. As far as Brock was concerned, there shouldn't be any confusion.

To Anya, Brock was nothing more than…

He shook his head. What was he to Anya? He didn't know how to begin to answer that question. How could that be? Weeks ago, when he'd first arrived in Aurora, everything was so clear.

Brock's head throbbed. "You two obviously have some things to talk about. I think I'm going to head out."

He turned to go.

"Wait," Anya called. "Don't leave."

Don't leave.

Her words sliced right through him. They made him want things he shouldn't.

He couldn't keep doing this. It was torture. If it was this hard to walk away from Anya now, how much harder would it be two weeks from now? Three?

He'd tried avoiding her. He'd tried not to kiss her. More and more, it was all he could think about. And now here he was, standing in her childhood home, meeting her mother. As if he was here in Aurora to stay.

I can't do this, he thought. *If I don't leave now, I might never be ready to go.*

He waved at Anya and her mother and slipped out the door and into the cold.

It was time to put an end to things once and for all.

"He sure left in a hurry," Anya's mother said under her breath.

An uneasy feeling came over Anya as she watched Brock close the door behind him. There had been something foreboding about the way he'd left so quickly. Then again, it wasn't as though Brock had ever been much of a social butterfly. She was probably only imagining things.

"Anya?"

"Yes?" She blinked and tried to refocus her attention on her mother.

"Who exactly was that again?" Her mother frowned at the empty space where Brock had so recently stood. "And what's this about your new job?"

"I've been hired as a member of the avalanche search and rescue team. I'm going to be an official part of the ski patrol." As she said it, she realized just how much she liked the sound of it. She couldn't help standing a little taller.

"Oh. Well, I can't really say I'm surprised." Her mother's lips curved into a wistful smile.

"Really?"

"It's obvious you've really enjoyed your volunteer work with the search team. I haven't seen you so happy in a long, long time." Anya's mother reached out and stroked a lock of Anya's chestnut hair.

The comforting gesture caught Anya off guard. How many times had she dreamed of those weathered hands brushing her hair, twisting it into braids like all her raven-haired cousins? To have her mother's hands stroking her hair now, after all these years, satisfied a yearning she'd given up on long ago.

But why was she thinking of such things now? She was a grown woman. "I didn't realize you'd noticed."

"Of course I've noticed. You're my daughter, Anya."

You're my daughter. Anya's eyes misted over.

"Those aren't happy tears." Her mother stopped stroking her hair. Her mocha hand moved to cup Anya's cheek instead. "Are they?"

Anya very nearly lied. A lifetime of feeling different, of sensing a wall between herself and the rest of her family had trained her to put on a happy face and pretend like everything was okay. Even when it wasn't. Like now.

She looked into her mother's eyes and saw nothing but unguarded love and affection there. And she found she could do nothing but answer with complete and utter honesty. "No, these aren't happy tears. I'm thrilled about my new job, but it means Brock will be leaving soon."

Her mother gave a slow, knowing nod. "Brock is the gentleman you were just speaking with? The one you were so upset about on the day of the Reindeer Run?"

"Yes." Anya's hands trembled. She shoved them in the pockets of her jeans. It felt strange to be speaking so openly with her mother. Strange, but nice.

"You care about him a great deal, don't you?"

That was the question, wasn't it?

Anya swallowed. "Yes. Very much."

Her mother's dark eyes grew more intense, urgent. "Have you told him yet?"

Yet? "Of course not."

"Why not?"

Was she serious? If anyone in the world could understand how difficult relationships were for Anya, it should have been her mother. "Because, Mom, I don't know if I can."

Her mother guided her to the sofa and sat down beside her. She wove their hands together—warm, brown fingers laced with Anya's porcelain ones. "Are you going to let him leave Alaska without telling him how you feel about him?"

Tears stung Anya's eyes. As much as she wanted to break free from the past and move on, one question haunted her. A question she'd never allowed herself to ask anyone. Not even God.

She leveled her gaze at her mother. It was time—at last—to get to the heart of the matter, the crux of everything. "Why does everyone leave me?"

A sob escaped her, and her mother wrapped her in her arms.

"Sweetheart," she whispered. "You've never been alone. I'm right here. And your father left me, not you. We were kids. He didn't realize what he was doing to you. I'm sure not a day goes by that he doesn't think about you and wonder what could have been."

Her words hummed through Anya's consciousness, growing louder and louder.

What could have been…

Her mother pulled back, held on firmly to Anya's chin and looked her square in the eyes. "Don't let the pain of your past make you wonder the same thing—what could have been—a month from now, a year from now. Don't do what I've done and shut yourself off from the world. You need to tell Brock how you feel. You owe it to yourself."

The humming grew louder, more forceful, pounding in time with her heart. "What if he leaves anyway?"

"You'll survive. I promise."

Such a modest answer, beautiful in all its simplicity. And undeniably true. All these years of guarding her heart. Where had it gotten her? Alone. That's where.

Anya squeezed her mother's hand. "Why haven't we ever talked like this before, Mom?"

"I don't know. But I think it's high time we did. What have we been waiting for?"

What have we been waiting for?

What have I been waiting for?

She had to tell him. She had to tell Brock how she felt before it was too late. He would probably still go, but at least she would have no regrets after he was gone.

And deep down, Anya knew it was far too late to worry about getting hurt.

Chapter Fifteen

❧

Anya stood on Brock's porch and took a deep, fortifying breath.

You can do this. He's the same man who bared his soul to you in a snow cave. There's nothing to be afraid of.

She was back at the place where it had all started. As her hand wavered, poised to knock, she thought about the first time she'd found herself at Brock's door. Who knew she'd end up falling for the man in the bear suit? It was crazy.

She made her knuckles rap on the door before she chickened out. Three quick knocks.

The church group had left her mother's house barely an hour earlier. She'd cleaned up the coffee, placed the paper cups in the recycling bin and showed her mom all the work that had been done outside. Her mother had grown a little teary-eyed when she'd seen the roof and the neat paths they'd shoveled through the snow in the yard. Anya had suggested she might want to accompany her to church on Sunday to thank everyone for their efforts. To her shock, her mother said she would. It would be the first time Anya had gotten her out of the house in as long as she could remember. Perhaps they were both ready to move on.

Still aglow with the success of the morning, Anya had taken Dolce back to the cottage and picked up the hat she'd knitted for Brock. Now seemed like right time to give it to him. It sat nestled in the inside pocket of her parka, right against her heart—which, at the moment, was beating quite out of control.

You can do this. Just say it—Brock, I have feelings for you.

She'd kissed him, for goodness' sake! Surely she could talk to the man.

The door swung open. The instant she saw Brock's face, she knew something was wrong.

"Anya," he said without a hint of pleasure in his voice. In fact, there was a particular brand of sadness in his tone that she'd never heard from him before.

Her stomach flipped. Whether from nerves or the sight of that ruggedly handsome face, she couldn't be sure. Even when he frowned like that, he was still the most beautiful man she'd ever laid eyes on.

"Brock." She swallowed. "Is everything okay?"

He opened the door wider, giving her a perfect view of his wide-screen television, still the only fixture in his living room other than the sofa. A reporter stood clutching a microphone before a cluster of white-capped mountains, speaking in a language Anya didn't recognize. Spanish maybe? But she didn't need to understand the words to know something horrible had happened. The flashing lights of emergency vehicles cast garish arcs of light across the scene's snowy backdrop, and helicopters circled the skies.

"What happened?" Anya asked, but she knew the answer before Brock even responded.

"Avalanche." An angry vein throbbed in his temple.

"Where?"

"Formigal. It's in the Spanish Pyrenees. I was there about a year ago and helped put their search program in place."

"Was anyone…?" She couldn't finish the question. She didn't need to.

"Killed?" He fixed his gaze with hers. Along with the pain and sadness in his eyes, Anya saw a heavy dose of guilt. "Yes. Three skiers. And one search and rescue worker, who I trained myself."

"Brock, I'm sorry." She reached out and touched his arm, anxious to give him what comfort she could offer. But he stiffened at her touch. "This isn't your fault."

He nodded as if he understood. As if he agreed, which he obviously didn't.

"The skiers were in a restricted area. They shouldn't have been there in the first place. Still, I can't help but think I could have done something, taught those guys one or two more things. Now one of their ski patrol members is gone." He pulled his arm away.

The space between them felt far wider than it was. Anya wished he would invite her inside. She wished she knew the right words to say. She wished so many things.

"You can't save everyone," she said, her voice breaking.

Brock's eyes narrowed defiantly. "I can sure try."

And she knew then that today wouldn't be the day she told him she was developing feelings for him. Clearly, he was in no shape to hear it. He looked like he carried the weight of the world on his shoulders, and Anya felt as though the avalanche in Spain had put a wall of pain between them as real as the devastating path it had cut through the mountain.

Her heart broke for him.

She glanced over his shoulder again, toward the scene of devastation on the television. But this time, her gaze snagged on something else—two suitcases, opened and half-full, resting on the sofa cushions.

She didn't want to believe what she was seeing. She blinked, and tears swam in her eyes as she spotted his bear suit neatly folded at the top of one of the stacks of clothing.

Brock followed her gaze and blew out a sigh. "Anya…"

She cut him off. "Are those suitcases?"

It was a stupid question. She was just so stunned, she couldn't think of a thing to say.

Brock nodded—a slow, reluctant dip of his head.

Anya's hands shook. She sniffed back her tears, and the grief that had reached out and grabbed her at the sight of those packed suitcases morphed into something else. Hot, unrelenting anger bubbled up in her with such a sudden intensity, it frightened her. "You're *leaving? Now?*"

He spoke without even looking at her. "In the morning."

She wanted to slap him. Never in her life had she wanted to slap someone across the face before—not even Speed. But the urge to do just that to Brock had her palms itching. She wouldn't slap him, of course. She still possessed a modicum of self-control. But she wanted to, with every fiber of her being.

This was different from the other times. He'd changed her life. She'd trusted Brock. She'd told him things she'd never shared with anyone before.

She was in love with him.

And by all appearances, he'd been planning on leaving without even saying goodbye. He had to know how devastating that would have been for her. Didn't he care?

She crossed her arms tight across her body, as if she could hold herself together and keep from coming completely apart. She just had one question for him. Everything hinged on his answer. "When were you going to tell me?"

All he had to do was promise her he would have said goodbye—that he would have found her and explained why he was leaving so suddenly. She could forgive him. She could make herself understand. The avalanche in Spain had obviously dealt him quite a blow, and he was still doing his best to come to terms with his past. She couldn't fault him that.

But he didn't make any such assurances.

He said nothing, which told her everything she needed to know.

Why had she thought things would be different this time? Now, more than ever, she should have been prepared. Brock had always been honest with her. He'd never pretended he was going to stay.

Then again, she never expected his leaving to be like this. She'd thought he would at least have the decency to tell her goodbye.

"I'm sorry," he said, as if those two words could fix everything, could put her back together.

Walk away, she told herself. *He's not thinking clearly. Neither are you. Just walk away before you say something you'll regret.*

But she was beyond the point of reason. The sight of those packed suitcases had reopened old wounds she thought she'd at last left behind. She just didn't have it in her to stand by and watch someone she loved walk away. Again.

This time, she would at least have the last word.

"I was wrong about you, Brock," she spat. "You're no hero."

Then she spun on her heel, wanting nothing more than to put as much distance as she could between the two of them. He could go all the way to Spain for all she cared. It still wouldn't be far enough.

Brock watched the television coverage of the avalanche in Spain until his eyes grew bleary. By the time darkness fell over Aurora, he could rattle off all the facts about the disaster as if he'd been there when it occurred. The skiers had been skiing off-piste, which meant they were on the wild, untamed side of the mountain. The area hadn't been groomed or checked for safety, and the weather over the whole region had been rated a level four—high risk for avalanche activity.

This tragic storm of circumstances had ended with four skiers buried alive. Only one had made his way out. Brock now knew their names, their hometowns and which of them had had wives and children.

The ski patrolman who'd perished had been a

newlywed. His wedding picture had flashed across Brock's television screen at least half a dozen times. Sure enough, the smiling groom in the photograph had been a man Brock had trained during his time in Spain. They'd worked alongside one another, laughed with one another, shared a meal of *pisto manchego* together in a pub high atop the Spanish Alps.

And now that man was gone.

Brock had hoped busying himself with the details of the disaster and memories of his time in Spain would occupy his thoughts and ward off the memory of the hurt in Anya's eyes when she spotted his suitcases.

He was wrong.

She was everywhere—in his thoughts, under his skin, in his heart. Right along with the snow. How was he supposed to choose?

He wanted to stay. He wanted it as much as he wanted his brother back. When he'd left Anya at her mother's house earlier that day, he'd had every intention of coming home and making the call he'd been avoiding for weeks. He'd even gone so far as to dial the phone number of the avalanche unit in Utah, letting his thumb linger over the call button for a prolonged moment before he finally pressed it.

He'd hung up after the first ring.

He'd been unable to do it. He just wasn't ready to go. And for a fleeting moment, he'd thought that perhaps he'd never be able to leave this place behind. Maybe—just maybe—he could stay here and make a life with Anya if she'd have him.

Then while his phone was still resting in the palm of his hand, it had lit up with a text message from a ski patrol buddy he'd once worked alongside in France.

Slide in Formigal. Three skiers dead. Plus one of our own.

Eleven words.

Eleven words that had changed everything.

He'd turned on the television and stared, transfixed at the sight of the mountain where he'd stood twelve months before. *That's not the same mountain,* he'd thought bitterly. The jagged peak on the screen was a different mountain altogether—one with a wide path of death and destruction stretching from top to bottom. The landscape in Spain had forever been altered.

So had Brock's plans for the future. He'd made the call.

"Brock, I was beginning to wonder if you were avoiding me," the voice on the other end had said from Utah.

"No, of course not," Brock had said.

"How are things going up in Alaska?"

"Great. Couldn't be better. The folks up here will be just fine after I've moved on." Who had he been trying to convince—Guy Wallace or himself?

"Are you ready to come to Utah and take a look around?" Guy's voice had been hopeful to the point of begging.

They need me there, Brock had told himself. He didn't have a choice. Not really. What would happen if he decided to stay in Aurora? Would he turn on the television one day and see a scene similar to the one in Spain being played out in Utah? At least he'd done *something* to help the people in Formigal. Four people had died, but one skier had been rescued. It had been little comfort. If the same thing happened in a place where he'd refused to go, he wasn't sure he'd be able to live with himself.

"Yes, I'm ready," he'd said.

"How soon can you get here?" There had been audible relief in Guy's voice.

"Is tomorrow quick enough?" Brock had begun dragging his suitcases out of his closet even before the call was completed.

Sherlock and Aspen had watched him, their heads tilted at identical, curious angles. Brock hadn't been able to stomach looking at them, certain that on some level they knew exactly what he was doing— running away from something, rather than toward anything. When Anya had gotten there, she'd seen right through him.

You're no hero.

Perhaps the dogs could too.

His actions had been guided purely by instinct.

The slide in Spain had reignited a fire inside him—one that even the thought of Anya's soft skin and lovely eyes couldn't quench. He couldn't stay in Aurora indefinitely. He'd trained the team. They were ready. The dogs were ready.

But there were still dozens of mountains scattered across the globe that weren't.

The logic didn't quite ring true, even to his own ears. But he couldn't bring himself to stop packing, to slow down and think things through.

Something was wrong with him. He was broken. Broken in a profound and permanent way, and he had no idea how to fix it.

And now he'd broken Anya's heart too.

He turned off the television, tossed the remote control on the floor and dropped his head in his hands. He could watch TV until the sun came up, and he still wouldn't be able to erase the memory of the hurt he'd seen in her eyes.

He'd been almost relieved when she'd gotten angry. Anger he could handle. He deserved every ounce of righteous indignation she could muster. She'd placed her trust in him. She'd shared her secrets with him, and he'd done the same. In the end, he'd disappointed her as much as the others. Maybe even more so. She had every right to be angry.

But that wounded look she'd given him the instant she'd figured it all out was simply too much. He'd never felt less heroic.

You can't save everyone.

Truer words were never spoken. He couldn't save everyone, even after a lifetime of trying. He couldn't even save himself.

He dragged himself off the sofa and climbed into bed. Sherlock and Aspen followed him, but unlike most other nights, they didn't curl up by his feet. They slept on their dog beds, facing the other direction. Brock was certain they knew he was leaving them.

He closed his eyes. Exhaustion settled over him like a heavy blanket. And on his last night in Alaska, Brock wasn't tormented with dreams of snow. Tonight he dreamed of Anya dressed in white lace, walking toward him and holding a bouquet of fresh lavender tied with a smooth satin ribbon.

Chapter Sixteen

Anya's feet crunched through a layer of fresh snow as she headed for the ski mountain the next morning. She'd risen so early, she'd decided to walk instead of taking her car. As it was, she'd still be the first to arrive at the ski patrol cabin.

She hadn't slept a wink. How could she after all the things she'd said to Brock? If he'd harbored any doubts about leaving town so suddenly, she was sure she'd put an end to them.

You're no hero.

She cringed just thinking about it.

She'd been hurt. But so had he. She could see it the moment he'd opened his door.

And now he was gone.

Anya wasn't sure she could believe it until she saw it for herself. She didn't think it would sink in until she sat at that table in the ski patrol cabin where they gathered before training sessions and failed to see Brock sitting beside her.

And what about Sherlock and Aspen? Where were they?

Her heart hurt. She'd even brought Dolce along this morning. She figured she could use the moral support.

Dolce trotted at the end of her leash as they made their way across the lakeside path that led from the Northern Lights Inn to the mountain. Every few feet or so the little dog turned her head to make sure Anya was still behind her.

When they reached the ski area and the forest surrounding the cabin, Dolce pinned her ears back.

"What's wrong? Do you hear something?"

Anya bent to pick her up, but just as her fingertips skimmed the fur on Dolce's back, a loud grunt echoed through the woods. Anya recognized the sound at once as a moose. She'd never been afraid of moose, having grown up in Alaska. Dolce, however, found it terrifying. The dog bolted in the opposite direction so fast that before Anya could react, the leash slipped from her hand.

"Dolce, wait!" A thread of panic wound its way through her as she watched Dolce scamper wildly through the trees. The snow was so deep that it appeared to swallow the little dog, leash and all.

"Dolce! Dolce!" Anya's frantic screams bounced off the trunks of the surrounding evergreens and echoed through the canyon.

She whipped her head around as her own voice

called out to her on all sides. She strained her ears, desperate for any indication of her dog's where-abouts. Nothing. Not even the tiniest yip.

How did this happen?

Everything had changed in a matter of seconds. Dolce was gone without a trace. Even her tiny paw prints were impossible to find. The path she'd cut through the fresh powder intersected with trails of other animals that called the forest their home—snowshoe hare, moose, elk and who knew what else. Anya followed the one that seemed to head in the direction Dolce had disappeared. It led to a clearing just above the base of the ski mountain—a good sign, in Anya's opinion. Dolce should be eas-ier to see out in the open, away from the clusters of evergreen trees.

She shaded her eyes against the bright morning sun and peered into the distance. It was a gorgeous day. The sky was clearer than it had been in weeks and stretched out in an endless streak of robin's egg blue so bright that it almost didn't look real.

Just as Anya thought she spied a faint movement in the snow off in the distance, a loud boom echoed across the clearing. Anya ducked, convinced that what she'd heard was a gunshot. Her chest vibrated with the force of the noise. It had sounded like a bullet hitting a plate glass window, which made no sense at all. Hunting wasn't allowed anywhere near this area.

The ringing in her ears ebbed but was followed by a deep rumble that she could have sworn she felt in the soles of her feet. Anya stood back up. Nothing appeared amiss as she scanned the area that spread down into the valley. But when she turned and looked behind her, she could no longer make out the crest of the mountain or the neat ribbon of the Black Diamond trail snaking its way uphill. Instead, all she saw was a tumbling wall of white barreling toward her with what was certainly the speed and force of a freight train.

Avalanche.

She might have even attempted to say it aloud. But the word stuck in her throat. She nearly gagged, but as the first chunks of hard-packed snow tumbled past her, she was able to shake off her initial shock and horror at what was happening. Everything within her screamed a single, death-defying syllable. *Move!*

She knew better than to try to run downhill. Outrunning something of this magnitude was impossible. She didn't make any definite decision whether to head left or right—time to evaluate her best option was a luxury she simply didn't have. Her moves were guided purely by instinct. She swiveled toward her left and began running as fast as she could.

If she could just make it back to the forest, perhaps she could find some sort of shelter. She ran as swiftly as her legs could carry her. But after only one or two steps, she tripped and fell to her knees. The snow was coming quicker now. There was no time—no time to think, no time to do anything.

Tears stung her eyes, and her breath came so fast, she was sure she was hyperventilating. This realization was the slap in the face she needed.

For weeks now she'd been training for a scenario just like this one. Granted, she'd never thought she would be the one to fall victim to an avalanche. The plan was for her to be the one coming to the rescue. But plans changed. And even though she'd been caught completely off guard and unprepared, there were things she could do to increase her chances of survival.

Think, Anya.

She didn't have a single piece of equipment with her—no beacon, no AvaLung, not even a shovel. She'd planned on picking up these regulation items once she reached the ski patrol cabin. But Dolce's detour had changed things. And here she was, within moments of being buried alive, with nothing—and no one—to help her.

Never will I leave you; never will I forsake you.

"Please, God," she cried. "Please."

And in the final, fleeting moment before the wall of white slammed into her, she remembered something Brock had once said. Something so simple and elementary, it had seemed like common sense at the time, barely worth mentioning.

When you arrive at the scene of an avalanche, search the debris field for clues. A mitten or glove poking out from the snow could help lead you to a victim faster.

Anya clawed at her mittens and tried to yank them off, but her hands were shaking so hard, it was hopeless.

God, please. There has to be something.

Then she remembered Brock's hat.

She jammed a hand into the inside pocket of her parka and there it was—right where she'd left it the night before, after their awful encounter.

She pulled the hat out and tossed it as high in the air as she could at the exact moment her feet were knocked out from beneath her. Its garish bright stripes and cherry-red pom-pom streaking across the clear blue sky were the last things she saw before she curled her body, closed her eyes and let the snow take her under.

Everything became little more than a blur. A blur of sound and sensation—the roar of the snow and the sense of being picked up and carried from one end of the world to another. There was no time to pray, no time to wonder if she would live or die. Because it seemed as if it ended as soon as it had started.

And then there was nothing.

The stillness and its accompanying quiet came about so suddenly that Anya found it almost as frightening as the noise. She lay still for several minutes, afraid to move and discover she'd been seriously injured. She attempted to wiggle her fingers first, then her toes before realizing even the tiniest movement was out of the question.

It was as though she'd been buried in concrete.

Don't panic. You'll waste precious energy.

At least she'd somehow managed to end up with her arms curled, trapping a decent-sized pocket of air around her. She had no idea which direction her body faced. Up? Down? Who knew? What mattered most was that she could breathe.

For the moment.

When she'd willed her heart to stop beating out of control, she opened her eyes and saw nothing but blue. This caught her by surprise. She wasn't sure what she'd expected. White maybe? Gray? But not blue. Blue, like the beautiful Alaskan sky. Blue, like a glacier floating in the ocean in summertime.

Blue, like Brock's eyes.

It was then, when she first allowed herself to think of Brock, that she began to cry. A sob rose up through her body from the depths of her soul. She wasn't even sure if there were actual tears. Her face was so numb and cold, all she could feel was the weight of snow pressing heavily against her cheeks. But she wept all the same.

Would she ever see him again?

She doubted it. Even if somehow, some way she was rescued, he'd already left Aurora. To make matters worse, she didn't even know where he'd been planning on going.

She was sure he was long gone by now. That's the real reason she'd come in early today. She'd fully expected to walk into the ski patrol cabin and discover he'd left. She'd wanted to face it as quickly as she could, like ripping off a Band-Aid, so she could forget all about him and move on. The only question that nagged at her was what he'd done with the dogs. He should have left them in her care, but after the dressing down she'd given him, he'd obviously taken them elsewhere.

Maybe he's still here.

Maybe he's still here, and he'll come for me.

It was too much to hope for. Anya couldn't even allow herself to consider the possibility that Brock would come to her rescue. After the things she'd said to him, how could she expect him to stick around and dig her out from under a pile of snow?

You're no hero.

Regret pierced her heart.

She should have given him the hat she'd knit for him. It was a ridiculous thing to cross her mind at a time like this, but she wished she'd given it to him. Because then she would have found the courage to tell him how she felt about him.

She was in love with him. If she'd been afraid to admit it before, she had no qualms about it now.

Imminent death had given her unwavering clarity. She was in love with Brock Parker, heart and soul.

Why hadn't she told him? Would it have changed things? Would he have stayed?

She'd never know.

And now she'd never have the chance again to say those words to him.

She'd been so afraid. And why? Look where being afraid had gotten her. She'd never been so completely or utterly alone in her life. Even Dolce was gone.

Anya felt her breathing growing shallow. She tried to move her head from side to side to widen her pocket of air. It took every ounce of strength she possessed, but eventually she heard crunching noises and her head was able to move a few inches. She could breathe a little easier. For now.

How much time did she have left?

She wasn't even sure how long she had been buried. Five minutes? Ten? Fifteen?

The first fifteen minutes are the most crucial for locating victims, she heard Brock say in her head. *At the thirty-five-minute mark, chances for survival drop to a mere thirty percent.*

She wished she didn't know these statistics. They made her feel like a ticking time bomb, ready to explode.

The worst part was knowing there was nothing

she could do but lie there and wait. She was completely helpless.

Helpless and alone.

Another sob wracked her body. She concentrated as hard as she could on God's promise—the one that had always had a way of speaking directly to her heart. *Never will I leave you; never will I forsake you.* And for the first time, she doubted those words.

She'd misread the signs.

She'd been so sure of God's plan. Everything appeared to lead to her becoming part of the avalanche rescue team. She'd thought it was her destiny. The signs. There'd been so many of them—Brock's arrival, working with the dogs, that Bible verse she'd found. What was it again?

Though the mountains be shaken and the hills be removed, yet My unfailing love for you will not be shaken.

She'd been convinced she knew what all the signs meant. Now she realized she was wrong. Everything that had happened had been leading her here, to this moment when she needed to believe in God's promises more than ever before. He wasn't trying to steer her in one direction or another. He wanted her to know that He was faithful. She wasn't alone at all. He was right there beside her. Even now.

Never will I leave you; never will I forsake you.

She repeated it over and over in her head, until at last she began to believe it.

* * *

The moment Sherlock raised his muzzle from the top of Brock's foot, where he'd been resting it for the past hour and a half or so, Brock knew something was wrong. Everything about the dog's body language—the pricked ears, the slight rise of his hackles and the widening of his eyes—spoke of imminent trouble.

Brock's knife paused midair. A single, slender ribbon of wood fell to the table. "Everything okay, bud?"

Sherlock remained perfectly still as he emitted an eerily high-pitched whine.

Brock had been at the ski patrol cabin since before the sun came up. He couldn't sleep—not after that dream he'd had. When he'd awoken in the early morning hours rested and content, he realized what a toll the years of nightmares had taken on him. It wasn't his only realization.

He couldn't leave Aurora. Not now and possibly not ever.

Brock was no fool. The fact that he'd dreamed of Anya instead of Drew meant something. Even though it had only been a product of his subconscious, the sight of her in bridal white had led him to see everything with sudden clarity.

He was in love with Anya Petrova.

And he intended to tell her the moment he saw her.

He'd slipped out of bed and headed straight to the

ski patrol cabin, hoping to catch her alone before everyone else arrived for training. He'd considered going to her cottage instead but thought better of it as he revisited the way he'd treated her the last time they were together.

She'd seen right through him. He'd been planning on doing the one thing that was sure to break her heart. He wouldn't blame her if she never spoke to him again.

He was certain showing up on her doorstep in the wee morning hours wasn't the right way to get back in her good graces. So he'd loaded up the dogs in the truck and driven to the ski patrol cabin instead. His suitcases still sat packed by his front door, but he no longer had any intention of taking them anywhere.

What had he been thinking? How could he have considered just up and leaving, even for a minute?

These were the questions that had been running through his mind all morning as he waited for her. He'd turned to whittling in hopes it would pass the time quicker.

He set the product of his work on the table and smiled. Even his hands could think of nothing but Anya. He'd whittled his best attempt at a matryoshka, more commonly known as a Russian nesting doll.

Brock had first seen them when he'd lived in Washington state for three months in a small mountain community with a large Russian population. The dolls were usually nearly cylindrical in shape, rounded at the head, nipped in at the waist and tapered toward the bottom. The largest one opened up to reveal a smaller one inside and so on. The one Brock had crafted for Anya was unique in that the smallest piece inside was a dog rather than a doll.

Perhaps he'd give it to her when he told her he loved her.

Now, however, Brock's thoughts turned to the matter at hand—Sherlock's odd behavior.

"What is it, boy?" he asked and ran his fingertips over the raised ridge of fur along the dog's backbone.

Sherlock didn't bat an eye in Brock's direction. Brock frowned and glanced toward Aspen, who'd been biding his time on the plaid flannel dog bed in the corner. Aspen, too, had alerted to whatever was causing Sherlock's distress. Like Sherlock, his ears stood high on his head, and he stared into the distance with an intensity that sent a shiver up Brock's spine.

He strode to the window and looked outside. Everything appeared completely normal. It was, in fact, a beautiful morning. The sky was clearer than it had been in weeks—clear, crisp blue rather than the disturbing gray–green that had so worried Brock before. And for once there wasn't a single snowflake in sight.

But Brock knew better than to ignore such obvious signs of alarm in the dogs. They'd heard something. It was probably only a sick or injured animal hanging around the outside of the cabin. He tried to shake off the feeling that it could be something more.

It was a commonly held belief that certain animals had the ability to predict danger—specifically, natural disasters—long before humans were aware of anything amiss. There were countless tales of elephants, cattle, dogs and all variety of zoo animals exhibiting odd behavior before earthquakes and tsunamis. Brock remembered reading an article in *Nature World* magazine in which scientists speculated this mysterious sixth sense was really a heightened state of hearing or had something to do with electromagnetic waves. Brock didn't really care how they did it. The bottom line was that he simply trusted his dogs.

And right now they were telling him in no uncertain terms that something was up.

He grabbed his parka off one of the hooks by the door and shrugged into it. His plan was to take a look around the perimeter of the cabin for signs of an animal in distress. He was sure he'd find a moose that had stepped in an illegal trap somewhere in the woods or perhaps an orphaned fox. He hoped it wasn't a wolf.

But as he gripped the doorknob, it trembled slightly in his hand.

He gripped it tighter, convinced he was imagining things.

It trembled again. And then came the noise.

No matter how many times he heard it, the sound of an avalanche never failed to fill him with equal parts awe and dread. Before he'd ever witnessed such a spectacle firsthand, he'd heard it described as sounding like rolls of thunder. In actuality, it was far more intense—like being *inside* thunder. And the rumble was typically preceded by a single, earsplitting explosion—the snowpack cracking under the pressure of whatever had weakened it to the point of giving in.

This time was no exception.

When the snowpack broke, Brock's ears rang. Sherlock and Aspen ran around the cabin in frantic circles, foaming at the mouth and barking. Not that Brock could hear them over the roar. It was so strange watching them bark like that, as if they were mute.

It's close, he thought, gripping the doorframe as the walls of the cabin shook. *Too close.*

He fought the powerful urge to run outside, and instead waited for the slide to end. After all, he couldn't help if he was buried himself. Still, he hated the wait. It felt like an eternity, even though in reality it was likely less than a minute.

The trophy he'd won in the Reindeer Run bounced right off its shelf and crashed to the floor, but then the earth stilled beneath Brock's feet and a deadly hush fell over the mountainside.

"Sherlock, you're coming with me." The dog sprung to Brock's side. "Aspen, stay. With any luck, Jackson will be here soon and he'll bring you out."

He pulled on his gloves, grabbed the ready-pack with his collapsible probe poles and snow shovel and did his best not to become weighed down by the pressing feeling that something was wrong. Very wrong.

As he crunched through the snow with Sherlock at his feet, he concentrated on the positives. It was still early morning—the ski area wasn't even up and running yet. The timing of the slide couldn't have been better. Chances were no one had even been on the mountain.

Then why did he have such a sickening feeling in his gut, as if none of these things mattered at all and he was about to face the absolute worst the snow had to offer?

Chapter Seventeen

In the distance, just beyond the trees, Brock spotted the debris field. It cut a wide path through the clearing at the base of the Black Diamond slope. A powder cloud hung over the area but was quickly dissipating, settling over the upturned snow in a fine layer of white dust.

He wove his way through the evergreens toward the clearing. He'd only taken two or three steps when Cole appeared at his side, puffing and wheezing for breath.

"What just happened?" Cole asked, his face ashen.

"Avalanche." Brock kept walking, unwilling to pause for even a moment, although it looked as if Cole needed a good shake.

"I don't understand. We've never had an avalanche here before." He shook his head, his eyes widening at the sight of the slide.

"Cole." Brock rested his hand on Cole's shoulder.

The gesture was meant to both reassure him and bring him back to the present—away from the jolt of what he'd stumbled upon. "This was inevitable. We're prepared. This is what we've been training for. This is why you brought me to Alaska. Right now, you need to get to the cabin and grab a ready-pack and Aspen. Got it?"

"Yes." He nodded, the color returning to his face slowly. "Yes, of course."

"Good. Hurry and get Aspen, then do everything exactly as we did in training."

Cole nodded. "Scan the area for clues first, then let the dog do his job. If he alerts, start digging. I'm on it."

Brock breathed a sigh of relief that another pair of able hands had shown up. He had no doubt Cole was more than capable of acting as Aspen's handler in Jackson's absence, especially now that he'd gotten over his initial shock.

As Brock had suspected, the entire area appeared quiet, as if the ski mountain had not yet climbed out of bed for the morning. Besides Cole, he'd yet to catch a glimpse of another person. The lift wasn't running, and though he could barely see the parking area from where he stood, it appeared to be empty. But just as he reached the edge of the tree line, he caught a movement out of the corner of his eye. Something small, close to the ground. Beside him, Sherlock shimmied with awareness.

Brock hastened his steps in the direction he'd spied the activity. And when he grew close enough to discern the outline of a small dog, he tensed.

No. The bitter taste of stone-cold fear rose up the back of this throat. *No, it can't be.*

"Dolce?" he whispered, the word sticking in his throat.

The dog quivered from her nose to the tip of her tail, which was tucked snugly between her two back legs. But her tail gave a tiny hint of a wag of recognition at the sound of his voice. And with that smallest of movements, Brock's world crumbled around him.

This was unquestionably Anya's dog.

Dolce's leash was attached to her collar, and it had somehow gotten snagged on an evergreen, leaving the poor dog cowering beneath the tree's low-hanging branches. But Anya was nowhere to be seen.

Brock struggled to catch his breath. His heart was beating nearly out of control. Anya had to have been there when the mountain gave way. As much as he didn't even want to consider it, deep down he knew it was true. She loved that dog. If Dolce was there, so was Anya.

Do something.

He felt sick, literally physically ill. How had this happened? This was exactly why he didn't let himself get close to anyone—he wasn't prepared to lose another loved one.

And he refused to lose one now.

Brock propelled himself into action. He wrapped Dolce's leash around the tree trunk two more times and pulled it tight, speaking in soft, reassuring tones to the frightened dog as he did so. "Don't you worry, little one. I'm going to find her."

He had to find her. Failing wasn't an option.

"Let's go, Sherlock."

Brock ran toward the clearing with Sherlock on his heels. Somewhere in the back of his mind a voice told him to slow down and breathe. He needed to conserve his energy for the dig. But he couldn't seem to make himself go any slower.

When they reached the debris field, he forced himself to come to a stop so he could look for clues to Anya's whereabouts. He shielded his eyes from the sun and couldn't help thinking how odd it was that his life had been reduced to tatters on such a beautiful morning. The bruised sky of earlier in the week was nothing but a memory now, but the heavy snow they'd had from the recent storms had undoubtedly contributed to today's disaster.

He swept the area with his gaze, praying for a glimpse of mitten…scarf…anything.

Please, God, please.

The settling powder cloud and the bright sunshine weren't helping matters. Glittering crystals swirled around him, obscuring his vision. Brock couldn't see a thing other than white. Snow was everywhere—

beneath his feet, hanging in a suspended cloud over his head and even in the air he breathed.

"Find Anya," he ordered Sherlock. "Find Anya."

At the sound of the familiar name, Sherlock's eyes lit up, and he let out a loud bark of recognition.

"Find Anya," Brock repeated, his voice growing hoarse.

Sherlock lifted his head. Brock could tell he was attempting to air-search for her scent. The dog trotted ten or twelve feet uphill, then doubled back. He went in another direction, turned a circle and once again returned to Brock. He cocked his head and released a frustrated-sounding whine.

Brock's hope took a serious hit. The dog was confused. And why wouldn't he be? Anya's scent was all over this mountain. They'd trained here as recently as yesterday.

What was taking Cole so long? And where were the others? He needed a probe pole team out here. He had no other choice. Without any clues and without any scent trail for his dog to follow, Brock hadn't the vaguest idea where to start. But Brock knew as surely as he knew the sky was blue that everything in his life had led to this morning—all the mountains he'd seen, all the training, all the rescues, all the piles and piles of snow. Now he knew. All the while he'd been preparing to rescue the woman he loved. He knew it down to his bones.

He also knew that despite a lifetime of preparation, he wasn't up to the task. He couldn't do it—not alone anyhow. There was too much at stake.

He sank to his knees, broken and desperate.

God, please. I need You. I know I don't deserve Your help, but she does. I'm begging You...

God had been chasing him since the day he set foot in Aurora. Brock knew that now. The church, the Bible in the ski patrol cabin, the woman with the violet eyes who'd found her way to his doorstep on that very first day. God had orchestrated all these events. And Brock had turned a blind eye to every one of them.

Had he really been so stubborn that it came down to this?

Yes, he had. But not anymore. He was done going it alone. He'd made a mess of things. He couldn't imagine how he'd lasted as long as he had without God.

I'm Yours. No matter what happens here, I'm Yours. But please help me find her.

He lifted his head and, off in the distance, he caught a glimpse of an unmistakable flash of red.

He scrambled to his feet and ran toward it, his thoughts screaming *thank You, thank You, thank You* as he went.

"Brock?" Cole called out from somewhere behind him. "Have you spotted someone?"

Brock had never been so happy to hear Cole's

voice. He'd take all the help he could get right now.
"Over here. Hurry!"

The flash of red grew closer. When Brock reached
it, he still wasn't altogether sure what it was—something knitted. A scarf maybe? He tugged at it and
realized it was a hat. A comically oversized hat, like
an old-fashioned sleeping cap, only with crazy mis-
matched stripes. Brock had never seen it on Anya's
head before, but it had her name written all over it.
So much so that he smiled as he reached inside his
pack for his snow shovel.

Sherlock's nose dropped to the ground, and no
more than two feet away from where Brock had
found the hat, the dog alerted. He barked, pawed at
snow and barked some more.

"Good dog," Brock somehow managed to say,
even though his throat was so thick with emotion
that he was rapidly losing his ability to speak at all.
"Good boy."

He speared the spot Sherlock had indicated with
his shovel. Cole appeared at his side the moment he
scooped away the first shovelful of snow. Brock was
so happy to see him, he nearly wept.

Cole took in the scene: Brock digging like there
was no tomorrow, and Sherlock digging too, almost
half-buried in snow. "Whoa! You two have found
a victim."

"Not a victim." Brock shook his head and heaved
another shovelful of snow over his shoulder. Some-

thing in him snapped. He couldn't take hearing her referred to that way. "Anya."

Cole froze. "Anya?"

"Yes, Anya."

Neither one of them said another word after that. They just dug and dug. Even the dogs dug. And all the while, Brock prayed like he'd never prayed before.

"I've got a foot," Cole yelled.

Brock turned and saw the familiar toe of one of Anya's snow boots. It wasn't moving.

Please, God.

His biceps burned from digging through snow as hard as concrete, but he plunged his shovel into the snow with renewed vigor. And when he lifted it up and away, he was rewarded with a glimpse of Anya's beautiful face.

"Cole, help!"

He threw the shovel down, tore off his gloves and began pushing the snow back from her face as fast as he could. Her eyes were closed, her lovely dark eyelashes coated with snow. Brock's chest seized. He couldn't tell whether or not she was conscious. He just hoped they weren't too late.

Once her head was fully exposed, Brock cradled her face in his hands. Her cheeks were freezing cold to the touch, but the moment his fingertips brushed across her skin, her eyes fluttered open—those violet eyes that never failed to take his breath away.

She was alive.

The sight of those familiar, lovely eyes peering up at him, shining with life, brought forth a gentle healing in Brock. He could no longer feel the broken place that had been inside him since he was a scared, lonely kid. Finally his soul had found rest.

She blinked, a slow sweep of her lashes. "Brock?" she whispered as he swept the snow away from her lips. "I was afraid you'd gone."

He shook his head, too full of emotion to speak. He cleared his throat and realized he was crying. He hadn't cried since Drew had disappeared. But he was crying now. Crying like a baby, in fact. And this time they were tears of joy.

Thank You, God. Thank You.

"Not me," he said, when at last he was able to speak. "I'm not going anywhere."

Anya had been sure she was dying.

It had started with a fierce burning in her chest and the accompanying urge to cough. At first she'd been able to resist it, too frightened to waste what precious little air she had left. But before long she just couldn't help it. She'd coughed once, twice, her heart beating furiously against her ribs, and she'd realized she was panicking.

The panic had passed quickly enough, replaced with a startling calm. She'd no longer felt the need to struggle for air. The tension had lifted from her body, and her eyes had drifted shut.

And she'd thought she was dying.

Then she'd heard the barking of the search dogs, and she knew with absolute certainty she would be rescued—that Sherlock and Aspen would find her. She'd just had to force herself to hang on until they did.

What she hadn't expected was that Brock's face would be the first thing she saw when the snow was pushed away and she opened her eyes. It was the most glorious sight she'd ever beheld—those chiseled features of his against the backdrop of a sky as blue and beautiful as his eyes.

For a fleeting moment she'd thought what she was seeing wasn't real. But then she'd seen herself reflected in his eyes, flooded with tears. And she'd known. It was real.

Brock had saved her. And now he was saying the words she'd so longed to hear.

"I'm not going anywhere."

Sherlock nudged his way in front of Brock and licked the side of her face. She laughed.

"Sherlock, bud. Let's give her some space." Brock pulled the dog away, but he kept his gaze fixed on her even as he checked in with Cole. "How's it coming with her legs?"

"Done."

She wiggled her feet. She could move. Finally.

Brock pushed the snow away from her chest, and at last she was fully free of the crushing weight of the snow. She inhaled a deep lungful of air. The oxygen burned her insides, and she coughed again.

"Take it easy, sweetheart. You're okay now." Brock's words were as soft as a caress. Hearing him call her sweetheart brought fresh tears to her eyes. And he lifted her into his arms, as if she weighed no more than a snowflake. "You're okay. I've got you."

"You gave us an awful fright, Anya." Cole looked more choked up than she'd ever seen him. "I don't know what we would have done if…"

His voice trailed off. There was no need for him to finish the thought. They all knew how it ended.

"Was there anyone else out here before the slide?" Brock asked. He was still holding her, cradling her in his arms. He didn't seem in any hurry to put her down.

"No." She shook her head. "There was no one."

Then she remembered how it had all started.

"I was looking for Dolce. A moose frightened her, and she got away from me. We have to find her. Put me down." She struggled to free herself from Brock's grasp. But she was no match for the strength of his arms. They kept her held firmly against his granite chest.

"I'll do no such thing. I don't intend to let you out of my arms for a long, long time. If ever. And don't worry about Dolce. She's fine. A little scared but fine. She's right over there." He nodded toward the tree line.

"I'll go get her. You two look like you could use a little privacy." Cole turned to go but not before Anya spotted the grin on his face.

"I think he knows," Brock whispered.

"Knows what?"

"That I'm in love with you." He smiled at her, and her chills instantly subsided. She felt warm, safe and loved in his arms.

She snuggled into his embrace. "Do you think he knows that I love you too?"

He laughed, and the sound burrowed under her skin. "Probably. Let's hope he knows and approves. Then maybe he'll offer me a job again. Because I'm not going anywhere, Anya. I mean that as surely as I live and breathe."

She let the truth settle over her like the softest of snowfalls. She was alive. Brock loved her. And he was staying. She'd thought she was dying, but instead she found herself more alive than ever before.

Thank You, Lord.

She smiled up at Brock. "You just pulled off an impossible rescue. I'm thinking that affords you some job security. How did you find me?"

"Your hat." He nodded toward the red hat, heaped in a puddle of stripes in the snow.

"What do you know? It worked."

"What worked?" He looked confused.

"I remembered what you said about searching for clues after a slide, and I tossed it up in the air right before I got knocked down. I'd hoped someone would see it and come looking for me." She wondered if things would have ended so happily if she'd forgotten she'd had the hat in her pocket. Would Brock have still found her? "And actually, it's not my hat. It's yours."

"Mine?"

"Yes, yours. I made it for you. I thought you could use a new socialization tool."

He rolled his eyes, but there was unmistakable joy in the gesture. "That crazy hat saved you, you know."

"No," she said, her vision growing cloudy from behind a veil of tears. "You are the truest of heroes, Brock. You always have been. *You* saved me."

"I'm afraid it's the other way around, sweetheart." His lips brushed against hers in a gentle, reverent kiss. "You're the one who saved me. You found me when I didn't even know I was lost. You and God."

"Is that so?" she asked through her tears.

"Yes. And now I'm staying right here. You couldn't get rid of me if you tried. And the first thing I'm going to do as an Alaskan is take you out on a proper date."

She laughed, still not quite able to believe she was alive and well and in Brock Parker's arms. "And then what?"

He set her down, then took her hands and anchored them around his neck. He gazed at her with eyes so earnest, she couldn't dream of ever looking away. "Then I'm going to ask you to marry me. What do you say to that?"

Everything within her radiated with joy. The danger, the past and all the hurt she'd ever experienced were forgotten. She knew only this day—the day she'd come to know just what it meant to trust God. And to trust her heart, her future, her very life to the man standing beside her, the man she'd one day call her husband.

She stood on her tiptoes to kiss him, and right before her lips touched his she whispered, "I say yes."

Epilogue

Three months later

Brock settled the squirming puppy—a little girl, who Anya had dubbed Watson because of the pup's fondness for Sherlock—onto the seat of the ski lift, inasmuch as a twelve-month-old Duck Tolling Retriever could be settled.

"You got her?" he asked his wife, a ridiculous smile springing to his lips as soon as the words were out of his mouth.

His wife.

Who knew a woman to come home to every night, to be his anchor after a lifetime of being untethered, would turn out to be the thing most worth searching for? Not just any woman, but this woman—Anya. He didn't need to travel the world to know that no one else could turn him upside down, inside out like she did.

"Yep. I've got a good hold on her. She's not going

anywhere." Anya bent to whisper in the puppy's floppy triangle of an ear. "You aren't going anywhere little one, are you?"

The puppy all but melted into a pool of adoration. As did Brock.

Anya glanced at him. "Come on up."

He climbed onto the seat, with Watson nestled snugly between him and Anya and gave the ski lift operator the thumbs up. Brock's feet lifted gently off the ground as they began the slow rise up the mountain.

It was early morning, hours before the ski resort would open for business. The rising sun peeked out from behind the Chugach Range, bathing the valley in a soft purple haze. The jagged peaks of the mountains were all but indiscernible, making it impossible to tell where the mountaintop ended and the violet sky began.

Brock cherished mornings like this, before the rest of the Aurora Ski Patrol arrived for work and he and Anya had time alone to work with the pups. Since his promotion to head of the unit, his days were often a blur of activity—he typically traversed the mountain countless times in a single afternoon. After the avalanche that had nearly stolen Anya's life, Cole had made the decision to take an early retirement but only after securing a promise from Brock that he would take over.

It was the answer to Brock's prayers—a way for

him to stay in Aurora with Anya yet continue to do the work that he still considered his calling, perhaps now more than ever before. He was responsible for the safety of everyone who set foot on the mountain, from skiers and snowboarders to his fellow ski patrol members. He could have never done it all without his staff, now composed of an impressive collection of search and rescue workers Brock had trained and worked with throughout the years, plus Luke and Jackson.

And Anya, of course.

He glanced at her now and found her grinning from ear to ear. Sometimes he marveled at his wife's bravery. It took a special kind of soul to go through a trauma like the one she'd been through and come out the other side. He'd encouraged her to take things slowly at first, to find her footing once again in the wild and beautiful world of Alaska.

Her mother had been a nervous wreck when Anya had announced only a day after the avalanche that she fully intended to resume her search and rescue work. In Brock's experience, tragedies had the polarizing effect of either bringing people closer together or driving them farther apart. Anya's brush with death had accomplished the former for her and her mother. Things had changed between them in a profound way. Brock's mother-in-law was even a regular at church now. Once or twice he'd even walked into the barn and found her there, reading to the puppies. As anxious as she'd been to repair her relationship with her daughter, she'd been less enthusiastic about Anya's increasing involvement with search and rescue work. Brock couldn't really blame her. He harbored his own concerns about Anya's safety.

They needn't have worried.

She'd become an integral part of the search team. And if that wasn't enough, she'd started a dog training program. His barn, *their* barn now, was full of pups of all ages—prospective avalanche dogs, search dogs being prepared for all kinds of scenarios and the odd timid stray. Brock wasn't even sure where she managed to find them all, but she was determined to turn their lives around, as she'd done for Dolce. Anya's little rescue dog, once terrified to venture from underneath the bed, now slept atop their bed every night, as content and happy as every dog should feel.

"Guess what I have in my backpack?" Anya asked, her eyes dancing.

"Another dog?" he teased.

"No, silly. A picnic."

"Only an Alaskan would consider a mountain-top picnic in subzero temperatures a good idea." He grinned. "I guess it's a good thing I'm an Alaskan now."

"It's the very best thing." She leaned over and cupped his face with her delicate hands.

He'd very nearly lost her. And God had led him to find her just in time. He would never forget what the Lord had done that day on the mountain. He'd spend a lifetime giving thanks and loving Anya with his whole heart as they continued their search and rescue work. Here in Alaska. Together.

Not because Brock felt he had to, not because he was still fighting old battles, but because it was his calling. He had a purpose here. And now that he was doing it for the right reasons, with the woman he loved by his side, he found he enjoyed it more than ever before.

"I love you, you know," Anya whispered as he bent to kiss her.

He murmured against the softness of her lips, "And I love you."

Anya's eyes fluttered open. As always, the full force of her violet gaze made him weak in the knees. She smiled at him. Then her gaze shifted. She glanced over his shoulder and let out a tiny gasp.

"Look, it's snowing." She pointed toward the horizon, where snowflakes were just beginning to float around the treetops in a glorious swirl of white. "Isn't it pretty?"

Brock looked up.

To anyone else, it may have appeared to be an ordinary snowy day in Alaska. Snow was nothing new here. It snowed more often than not in Aurora. But to him, there was nothing ordinary about it. Snowflakes drifted through the evergreens, gently falling from the heavens. For once, the sight of them failed to fill him with dread. The bitterness he'd carried with him since he was a boy was strangely absent.

Overcome, Brock lifted his face to the sky and let the snow dance against his skin, bathing him in a soft benediction. He was rewarded with a sense of wonder he'd never before understood he was missing.

A slow smile came to his lips as he realized what was happening. A change was taking place. One he'd never expected, even after all the Lord had done for him.

Finally he could appreciate what he'd been unable to see before. It had taken a lifetime for him to get here. But he'd made it. After all the heartache and restless searching—all the faraway mountaintops, all those he'd loved and lost—with his brave, beautiful wife at his side, Brock Parker could at long last see the beauty in a gentle snowfall.

* * * * *

If you enjoyed this story by Teri Wilson,
be sure to check out the other books
this month from Love Inspired!

Dear Reader,

Welcome back to Aurora, Alaska!

Alaska is a place where I'll always return, both in my writing and in real life. The beautiful scenery, quirky charm and independent spirit of the Alaskan people never fail to inspire me. From first sight, I fell in love with the state. The view of the snow-covered mountains from the airplane window looked like sugared icing on a cake, and I was hooked.

In *Alaskan Hero,* Brock Parker has traveled to countless faraway mountaintops as part of his job as an avalanche search and rescue patrolman. But Alaska is like no place he's ever been. And Anya Petrova is like no woman he's ever known. They both have painful pasts that make it difficult to open their hearts to love and the meaning of God's plan. Everything changes the day of the avalanche, and amid the dangerous beauty of an Alaskan winter, they come to realize love is the thing most worth searching for.

Avalanche search dogs and their handlers work all over the world, just like on the pages of *Alaskan Hero*. I was fascinated learning all about the important lifesaving work they do. I hope their bravery and dedication touch your heart, as well.

Alaskan Hero is the second book in my Alaska series. If you enjoyed Anya and Brock's story, I hope you'll check out the first book, *Alaskan Hearts*. And be sure to look for an Alaskan Christmas story coming this holiday season!

Wishing you all of God's blessings and peace,

Teri Wilson

Questions for Discussion

1. At the opening of *Alaskan Hero,* Anya encounters a man dressed in a bear suit. What kind of assumptions does she make about Brock based on his surprising appearance? How are these assumptions both correct and incorrect?

2. Brock plunges Anya into the world of dog training without explaining the tasks he's asking her to perform. What is your opinion of this teaching technique?

3. What incidents in Anya's past make her so determined not to give up Dolce, even though the dog's behavior may get her kicked out of her apartment?

4. Anya finds it difficult to have a meaningful conversation with her mother. Have you experienced such challenges with your mother? Why or why not?

5. Brock's job keeps him moving from one exotic place to the next. What do you think would be the advantages and disadvantages of this lifestyle?

6. What part of Brock and Anya's story hit home with you the most?

7. Anya has a strong emotional reaction when she first learns that Brock is only in Aurora temporarily. Do you feel that her reaction is justified? Why or why not?

8. Have you ever heard of an event like the Reindeer Run? Would you have participated in this event if you were there? Why or why not?

9. How does Anya's newfound faith in God impact Brock in this story?

10. Was the portrayal of Alaska in this story as you expected? Do you feel the Alaskan setting enhanced the romance between Brock and Anya? Why or why not?

11. What role do the dogs play in *Alaskan Hero?*

12. Why does Brock struggle with being labeled a hero? Do you consider him a hero? Why or why not?

13. Brock and Anya both have difficulty coming to terms with God's calling for their lives. Do you believe God has a specific calling for your life?

Why or why not? If so, when and how did you first recognize this calling?

14. What significance does snow play in *Alaskan Hero*? How does the symbolism of snow change as the story progresses?

15. What was your favorite part of this book?

LARGER-PRINT BOOKS!

GET 2 FREE
LARGER-PRINT NOVELS
PLUS 2 FREE
MYSTERY GIFTS

Love Inspired

Larger-print novels are now available...

LARGER-PRINT BOOKS!

GET 2 FREE
LARGER-PRINT NOVELS
PLUS 2 FREE
MYSTERY GIFTS

Love Inspired®
SUSPENSE
RIVETING INSPIRATIONAL ROMANCE

Larger-print novels are now available...

YES! Please send me 2 FREE LARGER-PRINT Love Inspired® Suspense novels and my 2 FREE mystery gifts (gifts are worth about $10). After receiving them, if I don't wish to receive any more books, I can return the shipping statement marked "cancel." If I don't cancel, I will receive 4 brand-new novels every month and be billed just $5.24 per book in the U.S. or $5.74 per book in Canada. That's a savings of at least 23% off the cover price. It's quite a bargain! Shipping and handling is just 50¢ per book in the U.S. and 75¢ per book in Canada.* I understand that accepting the 2 free books and gifts places me under no obligation to buy anything. I can always return a shipment and cancel at any time. Even if I never buy another book, the two free books and gifts are mine to keep forever.

110/310 IDN F5CC

Name	(PLEASE PRINT)

Address	Apt. #

City	State/Prov.	Zip/Postal Code

Signature (if under 18, a parent or guardian must sign)

Mail to the Harlequin® Reader Service:
IN U.S.A.: P.O. Box 1867, Buffalo, NY 14240-1867
IN CANADA: P.O. Box 609, Fort Erie, Ontario L2A 5X3

**Are you a current subscriber to Love Inspired Suspense books
and want to receive the larger-print edition?
Call 1-800-873-8635 or visit www.ReaderService.com.**

* Terms and prices subject to change without notice. Prices do not include applicable taxes. Sales tax applicable in N.Y. Canadian residents will be charged applicable taxes. Offer not valid in Quebec. This offer is limited to one order per household. Not valid for current subscribers to Love Inspired Suspense larger-print books. All orders subject to credit approval. Credit or debit balances in a customer's account(s) may be offset by any other outstanding balance owed by or to the customer. Please allow 4 to 6 weeks for delivery. Offer available while quantities last.

Your Privacy—The Harlequin® Reader Service is committed to protecting your privacy. Our Privacy Policy is available online at www.ReaderService.com or upon request from the Harlequin Reader Service.

We make a portion of our mailing list available to reputable third parties that offer products we believe may interest you. If you prefer that we not exchange your name with third parties, or if you wish to clarify or modify your communication preferences, please visit us at www.ReaderService.com/consumerschoice or write to us at Harlequin Reader Service Preference Service, P.O. Box 9062, Buffalo, NY 14269. Include your complete name and address.

LISLPDIR13R

ReaderService.com

Manage your account online!

- Review your order history
- Manage your payments
- Update your address

Enjoy all the features!

- Reader excerpts from any series
- Respond to mailings and special monthly offers
- Discover new series available to you
- Browse the Bonus Bucks catalog
- Share your feedback

Visit us at:

ReaderService.com

RS13